Daddy's Fake Fiancée

KELLY MYERS

Copyright © 2021

All rights reserved. No part of this publication may be reproduced, distributed, or transmitted in any form or by any means, including photocopying, recording, or other electronic or mechanical methods, without the prior written permission of the publisher, except in the case of brief quotations embodied in critical reviews and certain other non-commercial uses permitted by copyright law.

This is a work of fiction. While, as in all fiction, the literary perceptions and insights are based on life experiences and conclusions drawn from research, all names, characters, places and specific instances are products of the author's imagination and used fictitiously. No actual reference to any real person, living or dead, is intended or inferred.

Blurb

He's an aging actor... a *hot* aging actor.
And I'd be stupid to decline his tempting offer.

The arrangement is simple... or so it seems.

Chaz needs to be in the public eye to make himself known again.

And what better way to do it than have a young fiancée by his side?

That's where I come in.

I'll admit it – the fancy perks are nice.

But the best part about it is being close to him.

Falling for him wasn't a part of our contract.

And controlling my impulses becomes harder when I see him shirtless.

How is the simple young girl in me supposed to resist an older celebrity like him?

Yes, he's a playboy.

He's also been divorced.

And if all that wasn't enough...

He might have just used me. Big time.

It seems like running away is my only option.

But will I be leaving with my heart intact?

Chapter One: Taylor

After another long and grueling day of ballet classes, I walk up the pathway to Sunset Terrace, my apartment complex, and I'm relieved to be home. Ridiculously tall palm trees soar up on either side of me and, once again, I think about how much I love my little apartment.

Like me, most of my neighbors are young and chasing a dream. I live with actors, models, singers and surfers. But me? I'm a dancer. All I want, more than anything in this world, is to be a Prima Ballerina and dance in a prestigious company. So much so that I'm willing to sacrifice every other part of my life. I put my first pair of ballet slippers on at five and I haven't looked back since.

Now, at 22, after years of dedicated training, I am ready to start my career as a professional dancer and join a company. I've auditioned for two so far-- one in San Francisco and the other in San Diego-- and I've been on pins and needles waiting to hear back.

It is a huge accomplishment for a dancer to be accepted into a company. Ballet companies are made up in a hierarchical structure. Dance masters, artistic directors and choreographers sit at the top of the structure and the dancers themselves are divided into various levels. When dancers first join the company, they join the *corps de ballet*. They are the least experienced, appear least often and dance as a group during performances.

As dancers develop and start to command the spotlight, they become soloists. Soloists with a lot of experience and exceptional talent go on to become principal dancers. I am laser-focused on the top tier-- Prima Ballerina, the principal female dancer. It is a title of distinction that is awarded to very few dancers, but I know that I can get there. A title like that carries a great weight and I've been working all my life for it.

And nothing will stop me.

I unlock my door and step into my apartment. The walls are decorated with some of my favorite dancing posters from artists like Fabian Perez and Jack Vettriano. I drop my bag on a chair and head straight to the shower. I kick my flip flops off, strip out of my pale pink leotard and drop it in the overflowing hamper. More sweaty laundry to wash, I think. *Oh, joy.* It's literally never ending, and I hate doing laundry more than anything. If I don't scrounge up some quarters soon, my dirty clothes are going to get up and walk away.

I hit the shower and release the tight bun at the nape of my neck. Letting my long red hair down feels good and I massage my temples. Sometimes wearing it up and slicked back so much of the day gives me headaches. But now, I must get ready for the second part of my day, and I get to wear it loose and wild.

Ballet classes aren't cheap, and neither is living in Hollywood, so I work a few nights a week at a nearby nightclub called Club Noir. For a job, I suppose it's fun, but sometimes after dancing all day, the last thing I want to do is go dance another three or four hours. But the great thing about it is I get to shed the prim and proper look of a ballerina and embrace the fun, sexy side of me at the hip hop club. Ballet is full of intense and disciplined instruction so letting loose and just embracing the beat can be a nice change of pace.

I step out of the shower, dry off with a towel and then slip on a t-shirt and a pair of boxer shorts. I need to grab something to eat and head into the kitchen to search for something quick and easy. I throw the fridge open and frown. A lot of nothing stares back at me. I pull out some old Chinese food that my neighbor Jasmine and I got a couple of nights ago, lift the lid on the container, sniff and frown. *Eww. Nope.* I toss it in the trash and open the freezer. There's a frozen pizza and a macaroni and cheese in there. *So sad.* But I decide on the mac and cheese and pop it in the microwave.

When I realize I forgot to check my mail, I grab my key and head outside to the little row of mailboxes by the edge of the pool. The bright blue water glimmers and it's pretty quiet around here tonight. A lot of the tenants travel during the week, though, so it makes sense. But, when the weekend hits, we have barbecues and catch up on everyone's lives.

I unlock my little box, reach in and pull out a few envelopes. My heart stops beating when I see the correspondence on top with a return address that reads the San Francisco Ballet Company.

"Oh, God," I whisper under my breath. I auditioned for the company over five weeks ago and haven't heard a word since. *Moment of truth.* I take a deep breath and tear it open. My gaze scans down the short paragraph which thanks me for auditioning and then informs me that the company has finalized all their contracts for the upcoming season and that they could not offer me one.

"Fuck," I hiss. I tear the letter up and toss it in the small trash can nearby. With a sigh, I slump against my mailbox. I thought the audition had gone really well, too. The Assistant Director even complimented me.

Dammit.

Where did I go wrong? I had a letter of recommendation, took extra time with my appearance and made sure everything looked precise, clean and neat. I arrived early, warmed up thoroughly and I know I danced well. Maybe I should've been more up in the front? Or, had professional headshots and full body shots instead of the ones that Jasmine took?

All I know is rejection sucks.

I would've been happy getting into San Francisco, but whatever. Their loss. *Yeah, right.* I know it's my loss and I'm pissed. I work harder than anybody and I hate rejection. I know their ultimate decision depends on a variety of things such as individual attributes like perfect or nearly perfect body proportions, musicality and expressivity.

Ballet is an art based on not only a tradition of technique, but also of aesthetics and expressive qualities, so it's not easy to define who is the best or first. It's very subjective which is why a lot of dancers who have been granted the title of "prima" are controversial among aficionados. But the one thing they all do possess is distinctiveness and that's something that can only be achieved through natural gifts.

I know I have those gifts.

I must because if I'm not a ballerina then I have no idea who I am.

Whatever. Screw San Francisco. I try not to dwell on it too much because I'm still waiting to hear from San Diego about the audition I had there. The nice thing about San Diego is I'd be back home and close to my family. The bad thing is I'd be back home. For some reason, when people move away from their hometown and then return, they're looked at like failures. Like they couldn't hack it in the Big City, so they had to pack it up and go home.

As I walk back into my apartment, my cell phone rings, and I grab it. "Hi, Mom," I say. I try to sound cheerier than I feel.

"Hi, honey. How is everything up in LA?"

"Good," I say. *Shitty*, I think.

It's frustrating as hell to devote your life to something, believe it's what you're meant to do with your entire being and then have someone disagree and tell you that you're not good enough.

I pull the macaroni and cheese out of the microwave. It smells burnt and I peel the steaming plastic off it. Yep, it burned, but I'll still eat it. I put my mom on speaker as I dig in and she updates me on what my Dad and two brothers have been up to. I'm the oldest and my younger brothers are both still in high school. Johnny is captain of the football team and Bryce is a total tech geek who creates video games for fun. They couldn't be more different, but somehow it works and they're extremely close.

My siblings and I have a fun, teasing relationship and even though we like to pick on each other endlessly, we're a close trio and support each other hardcore.

When my mom gets around to asking if I've heard about either audition yet, I tell her no. I know it's a lie, but I'm scared that if I tell her the truth then I'm going to get a lecture. Despite my little white lie, I still get the speech that's becoming more and more common, and it grates on my nerves.

"Honey, we know how much you love ballet, but it's okay to have a plan B. I'm not saying give up on your dream, but maybe it wouldn't hurt to think about applying to colleges."

Fuck that, I think. "There are a lot of ballet companies, Mom. I've only tried out for a couple, and I will find the right one. It just takes time."

I know my parents have my best interests at heart, but the idea of throwing away 17 years of hard work makes my gut twist. What would I study, anyway? Business? Philosophy? Psychology? *Yawn*. I can't be trapped behind a desk all day, or I would die of boredom.

We talk for a few more minutes and then I tell her I must get ready for work. "I hate the idea of you dancing at some club and until so late at night, Taylor. Isn't there some other job you can find?"

My eyes slide shut. "No, Mom. I take classes all day, so I need something at night." I've explained this before, but it never seems to quite sink in completely. I know it's because she cares, though, so I just bite my tongue and listen to her other familiar speech.

"Maybe at a grocery store or the mall? On the weekends?"

I tell her that I'll think about it-- another lie-- and say goodbye. I feel bad, but I just don't want to hear it. In all honesty, I'm starting to get worried that my dream isn't panning out the way I want and it's enough to make me physically ill.

Great. Now I'm in a bad mood and must put on a smile and dance for the next few hours. I suppose it's the best thing for me, though. Go and lose myself in the music. I can forget about technique and style and my pointe shoes and, instead, just feel. I'm going to dance my anger and frustrations away tonight.

Back in the bathroom, I sit up on the counter and start to apply my makeup. I barely wear anything during the day except a tinted moisturiser and a little mascara. But, for Club Noir, I go all out with dark, smoky eyes, sparkles and a bold lipstick.

Same goes with my hair. Normally, it's up in a tight bun, but now I can use the curling iron to add some body and let it cascade down my back in red waves. Because I'm a ginger, my skin is porcelain. Sometimes it looks so milky-white that I feel like I'm glowing. But the strong sun here in Southern California is not my friend and I found that out the hard way after burning a few times. Now, I slather on the sunblock, especially when we have our pool parties and barbecues.

I'd give anything to have my neighbor's skin. Jasmine Torres has this perfect shade of golden-brown skin that looks perpetually tan and glows. Combined with her silky, straight, dark hair, almond-shaped eyes and statuesque figure, she's a knockout. And a very successful runway model. Right now, she's walking a catwalk somewhere over in Europe, but she promised to be back this weekend for the barbecue. I'm looking forward to catching up with her and my other neighbors, Hailey and Morgan.

Hailey Lane lives with Ryan Fox, the owner and landlord of Sunset Terrace. She's also a very talented singer and I know it's only a matter of time before she's slinging out hit records. Already, she has an agent and is meeting lots of important people in the music Industry. And, she hasn't even been out here for a year yet.

Ryan, or Foxy Flyboy as we like to call him, fell in love with Hailey when she moved in a few months ago. He's a hot, former military pilot and they are inseparable. Even though he's older, they're perfect together. Sometimes, when I watch them laughing or whispering or kissing, a part of me is a little envious. I've never had a serious boyfriend and I have no time to date. Besides, most of the guys I know are either gay ballet dancers or silly frat boys like my upstairs neighbors, Cody and Mason.

And I'm looking for something a little different. I slide off the counter and go down to my bedroom to get dressed. When the time comes, I know exactly what I want in a man-- and, at the top of that list is someone who will respect my career and give me the freedom and independence that I crave. I'm no one's arm candy and I have a mind of my own.

An older man will probably be best for me. Someone like Ryan Fox or Nick Knight. Savannah Hart, my old neighbor, was a model when she met Nick. He photographed her for a huge campaign, and they eloped in Las Vegas after knowing each other for a day. Talk about an impulsive decision, but when you know, you know. Now, she's four months pregnant and expecting twins. I'm so happy for them and I don't think that you can put a timestamp on falling in love.

It seems like all the younger girls here are being swept up in a whirlwind romance with an older man. *Good for them*, I think, and slip into a pair of extremely short, ripped up jeans. The front pockets are longer than the actual shorts and I pair it with a tank top and long-sleeve netted, mesh shirt. Then, I pull on my combat boots.

Yeah, when I decide to find a man, and that won't be anytime soon, he will have to understand my rigid schedule and how important ballet is to me. It's literally everything and I can't imagine a man ever being more important.

Is that weird? Maybe something is wrong with me. After all, I am a 22-year-old virgin who has no desire to have a serious relationship with anyone except my career.

But what if my worst nightmare comes true? What if I don't get into a ballet company?

No, I must stay positive and keep working hard. Keep striving for perfection. It's the only way I'll achieve my dream.

But, in the meantime, I'm going to burn off some stress, climb up into a wire cage and drop it like it's hot.

Chapter Two: Chaz

Here we go. I lean forward, fully expecting to hear an offer to star in the studio's action film, but instead, my agent squirms in his seat, suddenly looking very uncomfortable.

I lift a brow and wait while Cal Morris fidgets some more, plays with his napkin and finally clears his throat and makes eye contact. "So, they do want to offer you a role, but…just not the one you want."

Is he joking? I always get the role I want because I'm a fucking movie star who has paid his dues and worked in this town for a very long time. People respect me, cater to me and go out of their way to make sure I'm happy. I've earned it.

"What role?" I ask, completely puzzled. If it's not the lead or part of an ensemble with a group of esteemed, award-winning actors, why would I even bother?

"Lenny Lawrence," Cal says carefully, looking as though he hopes I don't remember the character.

Oh, but I do. I remember him quite clearly and I don't know if I am more insulted or livid. "The *grandpa*?" I burst out.

"Okay, I know. But, Chaz, you must understand that people's perception of you is changing. As fantastic as you look from all those hours in the gym, people in this town know you're of a certain age and that means the roles are going to start changing."

"I'm forty-fucking-two. Not 72. Do I look like I should be playing someone's grandfather?"

The more I think about it, the more pissed off I get. I eat right, work out five days a week and have the lightest touch of silver at my temples. The *lightest*. Like you need a damn microscope to see it. And the fact that my hair is a burnished golden-brown hide that silver damn well. Or so I thought.

"No, of course not," Cal soothes me. "They're idiots. But this is a huge film which means a wide-release and a big pay day for you."

And you, when you collect your ten percent, I think. Irritated, I grab my sparkling water with lime and take a drink. "I've made that studio millions. And now they think they can screw me over and insult me like this?" My eyes narrow. "Who are they eyeing for the lead?"

"Some new kid hot off a Netflix series."

I make a sound of disgust. *Figures.* "Tell them I said they can go fuck themselves."

"Chaz, I'm sorry, but you know how this town can be. Hell, be glad you're not a woman. They're past their prime by 30. The thing is, everyone knows you're over 40 and they're worried you won't be able to handle the action. It's going to be demanding and require months of training and-"

"*What?*" I practically roar. People sitting at the tables closest to us glance over and start to whisper. *Yes, this is where Chaz Stone has a total meltdown in front of the whole damn restaurant,* I think.

"That's the studio's concern," Cal says in a low voice.

"Did they have that same concern for Keanu Reeves when his 55-year-old ass did the latest Matrix? Or, for Sylvester Stallone and company when they filmed Expendables 15 or whatever number they're on? Jesus Christ, Cal. It's bullshit and you know it."

"I know, man, and I'm sorry."

"So, talk to them. Do your job, earn your ten percent and get me the fucking lead role. Otherwise, they can kiss my-"

"Chaz, please. This is Hollywood. One gray hair on your head and they're looking at you for an older role."

I decide I'm calling my hair stylist and booking an appointment to get my hair colored. I don't understand. Hell, I thought I was aging damn well. Am I the only one?

"This isn't a bad thing, you know. It happens to everyone. Eventually, you'll start playing more mature, fatherly figures. Look at Deniro. One of his best roles was in Meet The Parents."

"Yeah. Not Meet The Grandparents."

Cal swipes a frustrated hand through his hair, knowing he can't placate me and seeing his big pay check dissolve before his eyes. I deserve the lead role and if I can't have it then I'm not going to be in the movie.

"So, you want me to tell them no?" he asks.

"I want you to fight for me, Cal. Convince them that I'm the right actor. Not some fucking kid who probably just moved out here from Bumfuck, Iowa. Think you can do that?'

He loosens the tie at his throat and doesn't look as confident as I'd like. "I'll try, Chaz."

I push my chair back and stand up. "Don't try, Cal. Just do it."

Before he can give me another excuse, I walk away and head out of the restaurant. Out on the sidewalk, I hand the valet my ticket and take a moment to breathe deeply and collect myself. *You're 42*, I remind myself. *You're in good shape, probably the best you've ever been in, and that conversation in there was totally ridiculous.*

Grandpa. For fuck's sake.

I shake my head, starting to get pissed off all over again. When the valet pulls up, I slip him a tip and get into my silver Mercedes-Benz McLaren SLR. I'm feeling really grumpy and need to vent so I pull up my brother's number and connect the call.

"Hey, bro," Brand greets me in his usual cheery voice.

Brandon Stone is two years younger than me and my best friend. He helps keep me grounded and reminds me not to take all the Hollywood B.S. too seriously. And I love him to death for it. Without his unflappable support, I probably would've been on one of those sensationalistic shows by now that chronicled my depression and downfall into alcohol and drug abuse.

"Hey, Brand. I'm about ready to blow a gasket."

"What happened?"

"You know that role I wanted?"

"The action script you just read?"

"Yeah. Well, Cal just told me they want to offer the lead to some up and comer instead."

"That sucks," he commiserates.

"That's not even the worst part." I take a deep breath and then blurt it out. "They want me to play Lenny Lawrence, his grandfather."

There's a moment of silence and then my younger brother hoots with laughter.

My eyes narrow. "It's not funny," I tell him, hands clenching around the steering wheel.

It takes Brand a minute to compose himself and I can imagine the tears streaming from his blue eyes. "It's ludicrous," he says. "But this town is nuts. You know that."

Okay, I feel a little better. I can always count on Brand to help me get my head back on straight. "Because I don't look like a grandpa, right?" I need to hear it. I need the reassurance that I shouldn't be in a movie where someone is pushing me around in a goddamn wheelchair.

"C'mon, Chaz. You're 42 and could still pass for 32. Don't let those idiots get in your head."

I let out a sigh. "Thanks, bro."

"Look, why don't we get the entourage together tonight and go out? Just blow off some steam and have a few beers?"

Yeah, that's exactly what I need, I think. Thank God, for my little brother.

At ten o'clock, I walk into Club Noir with Brand and a few friends. John works as a talent agent and we met way back in the day when I first came out here from Buffalo, New York, to pursue acting. We used to crash on each other's sofas in between jobs when cash was low.

Oscar, or Ozzy as we call him, is a dance choreographer who puts together all the routines for the biggest pop stars in the world. He's always on tour with some boy band or pop princess so it's nice to see him tonight.

And Langston is the best entertainment lawyer in the business and the smartest man I know.

A cocktail waitress leads us over to the VIP section of the club. It's up on a dais in the shadowed, upper corner of the room and we all sit down and order a round. I can't remember the last time we all went out together so I'm really looking forward to catching up.

"It's been a while," Ozzy says with a bright-white smile and leans back in his chair.

"That's because your ass is always out on the road," John says. "Who's the latest pop superstar you banged?"

But Ozzy just shakes his head. "I don't bang them; I make sure it looks like they can dance. And, trust me, that's not always an easy job."

We laugh.

"What about you, Lang? Any women in your life or are you so buried in the books that you're going on your 5th celibate year?"

Langston flips John off. "For your information, I met my African Queen last month and I am anything but celibate."

The waitress brings our drinks, and we raise our glasses and toast Langston. "Spill it," I say. "Who is the woman who finally caught your fickle attention?"

"Her name is Nichelle, she's an ER doctor and I met her when I sliced my finger open on my letter opener and needed stitches. Her bedside manner charmed me, and I asked her out. We've been inseparable ever since."

"Good for you," Brand says.

"Fickle," Langston scoffs. "You should talk, Stone. You haven't had a relationship since Sabrina."

"That's because my ex-wife is a first-class bitch who taught me that happily-ever-afters only exist in the movies."

"So jaded," Langston says and sips his bourbon.

"How can I not be?" I ask. "Sabrina Destin was toxic and I'm lucky I got away with my dick still intact. Because she's the type who would've pulled some Bobbitt shit while I was sleeping. The woman was psychotic."

Brand laughs. "She really was," he agrees. "You guys should've seen it when we got back to their house after a fight, and she'd thrown every one of his belongings in the pool."

"My Golden Globe was in the deep-end, practically caught in the pump."

They laugh, but I just roll my eyes. I have no fond memories from when I was briefly married to Sabrina Destin. Also an actor, we met on set during a shoot and began a torrid affair. After a few months, we eloped, and it was the biggest news in entertainment. For a hot second, anyway. It didn't take long for her true colors to come out, though, and after only five months of marriage, I found out that she cheated on me with her newest co-star.

I told her I wanted a divorce; she flew into a rage and I moved out. It was a nightmare and the press hounded us, hoping for a public blowout. She loved the attention, whether good or bad, and always tried to rile me up. The entire thing was exhausting and since then, I avoid relationships and all the drama that comes with one.

Women are not worth it, I think, and look over to the stage where a large cage hangs in the corner. It was empty, but now I see a girl in little denim shorts climb up the steps and get into it. She tosses her long, fiery hair and begins to dance, moving that lithe body of hers to the beat. She has pale, almost translucent-looking skin, which tells me she's a real redhead. I like things that are genuine because I work in an Industry where everyone and everything is fake.

I can't look away. The way she moves draws me in, makes me wonder who she is and I want to know more about her. What's her name? How old is she? She looks young, but she possesses a confidence that captivates me.

"Okay, so why are we here hanging out with a bunch of 20-year-olds?" John asks.

"Yeah, who picked this place?" Ozzy looks around and frowns. "I feel like I'm at one of my boyband concerts."

"I did," Brand admits and looks over at me. "Our boy over here was feeling a little depressed about his age earlier today so I thought this might help cheer him up."

"Mid-life crisis?" Langston asks.

I shake my head. "Just a work-related thing," I say evasively and give Brand a look that warns him to shut the hell up.

"He got offered a role," Brand says a little too gleefully. "To play a grandpa!"

All of my so-called friends roll with laughter, and I glare at my brother. "It's not funny and I'm still pissed about it."

"A grandpa?" Ozzy slaps a palm against the table and doubles over.

"Hell, I know we're getting up there, but that's harsh," John says, but I can see the amusement glinting in his eyes.

"It's bullshit and I told them to fuck off."

"Good for you."

"Yeah, you tell 'em, gramps!"

I want to punch my brother, but instead I find myself looking back over at the pretty dancer in the cage. *Damn, she can move.* The guys must notice because they immediately start in on my new infatuation.

"You're drooling, Big Daddy," Ozzy says. "Or should I say Big Grand-Daddy."

They all laugh, but I ignore him. Why wouldn't I be drooling? She's gorgeous and something about her attracts me. It's a feeling I haven't had in a while and she's intriguing the hell out of me.

"You know what they say about redheads? They're feisty and headstrong," John says.

"I could use a little feistiness in my life," I murmured.

The guys all exchange an amused look. Then, Ozzy finishes his drink and snaps his fingers in front of my face. "Hey, over here."

I frown and pull my attention away from the redhead. "What?"

"How about a little bet?"

"What kind of bet?" I ask, instantly suspicious. Ozzy loves to stir shit up and I'm instantly wary.

"If you can't seduce that little redhead in one week then you accept the grandpa role in that movie." He sits back and smugly crosses his arms, waiting for my reply.

Dammit. You don't turn down a bet with your friends or you look like a pussy. "Fine," I say without giving it much thought and I shake his hand. I refuse to do that role and I want to get to know the beauty up in the cage a whole lot better so why the hell not?

Besides, I'm Chaz fucking Stone and I always get what I want.

Chapter Three: Taylor

After a couple hours of dancing, I am feeling hot, tired and in need of a break. I climb out of the cage, snag a cold bottle of water from Joe, the bartender, and head out the side door of the club. A cool breeze hits me and it feels like heaven as it blows through my mesh shirt. As I crack the water open and take a long sip of a much-needed drink, the side door opens, and a man steps out.

He looks over at me and pauses.

Ugh. Just keep going, buddy, I think. I only get 15 minutes to rest, and I don't like being bothered. Especially when I'm here working and it's usually some drunk idiot who tries to hit on me. Just because I dance in a cage doesn't mean I'm an easy lay. I should just hang a sign around my neck that reads, "I'm a virgin and it's not gonna happen so keep walking."

"Hi," he says.

Here we go. I struggle not to roll my eyes and finally look over at the person who's interrupting my alone time. And my heart kicks up a notch. He's older and incredibly good-looking. Not at all what I expected.

"Hi," I say, voice wary. He takes a step closer and the light above the door falls on him which gives me a better look. He's tall with dark, dirty-blond hair and a nice tan. His leading man looks leave me a little breathless and my gaze moves over the fitted Henley that hugs his broad chest. No denying the muscles hiding beneath it and my stomach does a little flip.

"What's your name?" he asks.

"Taylor. What's yours?"

For a second, he looks surprised that I asked. Then, he gives me a little smile and holds his large hand out. "I'm Chaz."

I shake it, not sure what to say, and feel a little zing shoot up my arm. For some reason, he looks familiar, but I have no idea why.

"You're a very good dancer," he says and releases my hand.

I notice the light scruff on his face and the smile lines at the corners of his blue eyes. "Thanks." He's a little too old to be hanging out at Club Noir and I wonder if he knows the owner or something.

"Any chance I can buy you dinner?"

Well, looks like Chaz wastes no time. "I don't think so," I say. "But thanks."

"Do you have a boyfriend?"

I hesitate. Then, nod. "Yep."

From the look on his face, he doesn't look convinced or deterred. "That's too bad. For him," he adds.

"Wow. Arrogant much?" I ask and place a hand on my hip.

"It's not arrogance," he assures me. "It's confidence. And, if you really do have a boyfriend, I'm not overly worried."

"Maybe you should be."

When he takes a step closer, my pulse skyrockets. "What's his name?" he asks in a low voice.

My mind goes blank. I open my mouth to respond, but nothing comes out, and I just look up into his eyes. They're beautiful-- a brilliant cobalt outlined in a darker shade of midnight.

The corner of his mouth curves up. "That's what I thought."

My gaze drops to his self-satisfied smile, and it irks me. "Cody," I inform him in a superior voice. Okay, so maybe Cody is only my upstairs neighbor and a total frat bro surfer who I am only friends with, but Mr. Hotshot doesn't need to know that.

When I see doubt flash through those eyes, I smirk. It feels good to knock him down a peg or two.

"Excuse me," I say and circle around him. "I have to get back to work."

Feeling triumphant, I head back into the club. Instead of going up into the cage, I climb up on a platform on the side of the room near the VIP section. I let the music take control and surrender to the rhythm. A few minutes later, I feel like someone's watching me and I notice a group of men sitting at a table in the VIP section.

And all five of them are staring at me, including Chaz. I have no idea what they're saying, but his friends seem amused. Maybe he told them that he just got shot down. I give my long hair a toss, swivel my hips and push Chaz out of my head.

Easier said than done, though. I can't deny that he's good-looking and I felt an instant attraction when he shook my hand out in the alley. That never happens to me. I am normally so consumed in my ballet goals that I never pay attention to men. Against my better judgement, I look back over at him.

He's staring, watching me intently.

My stomach drops and our gaze's lock. I swallow hard and force myself to turn away. *Holy crap*. He's looking at me like he wants to devour me. Maybe I should feel insulted, but I don't. To be honest, it's kind of turning me on. No one has ever looked at me with such intensity before.

This goes on for the next two hours and when the club lights finally turn on and they start kicking the stragglers out, I find myself turning back to his table. But he's gone. A part of me is instantly disappointed while the smarter side of me knows it's for the best.

I head backstage, grab my bag and slip out the rear exit. After I wave goodbye to a couple of co-workers, I make my way around the building to catch an Uber out front. I stop short when I spot Chaz leaning against the wall, as though he's waiting for me.

But he faces the other way and doesn't see me yet. As I debate whether I should do an about-face and slink away, a small group of giggling girls approach him. They're whispering furiously and have cell phones up, ready to take pictures.

"You're Chaz Stone, right?" one asks.

Chaz Stone? No wonder he looked familiar. He's only been in like a hundred movies. Thing is, I'm not a huge fan of action films so I'm not sure I've ever seen anything of his. I watch him push off the building and stand up. As he starts to sign autographs and take pictures, I decide to walk right past him. Of course, with the intention of completely pretending that I don't see him.

But I am curious and, as I pass, our gazes connect. His blue eyes widen slightly when he sees me, but I just keep walking. The last thing I want to do is interrupt. But, less than ten seconds later, I hear someone jog up beside me and turn to see him.

"Taylor, wait up," he says.

There's something sexy about his voice. It's deep, compelling and makes me want to sit down and talk to him. Yeah, me and a million other women in this world. Now that I know he's a famous actor, he is most definitely off-limits. They are the biggest playboys around. He may as well have "heartbreaker" stamped across his forehead.

"Where are you going?" he asks.

"My boyfriend's." It's a lie, but so what?

For a moment, he doesn't say anything, but I sense his energy deflates a bit. "Any chance you're contemplating a break-up in the near future?"

He sends me a dazzling smile and I can't help but shake my head and chuckle. "You are persistent, aren't you?"

"Oh, you have no idea. When I see something I want, I pursue it until it's mine."

I am the exact same way. I stop in my tracks and look up at him. "And, what in the world do you want from me?"

"How about a date?"

"Why?" I ask, full of suspicion. "You certainly don't seem short on female companionship," I add, referring to his group of fans.

"Because you intrigue me."

I turn and start walking again. I could say the same for him, but I don't comment. "You don't even know me."

"But I'd like to," he says in a low voice and touches my arm.

Again, that zing of sensation pings through me and I bite down on my lower lip. What is it about him that makes my heart skip? "I don't have time to date," I inform him.

"How does your boyfriend feel about that?" he asks teasingly.

I pull my arm away, hike my bag higher on my shoulder and start walking again. I feel my cheeks redden and for someone with skin as pale as me, it's the kiss of death. When I blush, there's no denying or hiding it. "I don't have a boyfriend. Happy?"

"Actually, yeah," he says, and I can't help but roll my eyes.

He's incorrigible.

"So, why don't you have time to date?" he pressed.

We stop at a crosswalk and wait for the light. "Because I'm a ballerina and my main focus is getting accepted into a ballet company right now."

"Really? How long have you done ballet?"

"All my life. It's all I've ever wanted."

"And so your job at the club-"

"Pays the bills. Not my dream," I add with a smile.

He seems to consider my words for a minute, and I can almost hear the gears turning in his head. But I have no idea what he could possibly be contemplating. When the sign turns to walk, I start across the street, and he stays right next to me.

"I assume you live close by?" he asks.

I nod. "Right around the corner."

"I hope you don't always walk home alone at 2am."

"I'm not alone," I say.

I notice his mouth edge up and then we turn onto a quiet side street. A cute sign announces Sunset Terrace and I stop.

"Home sweet home," I tell him.

"Can I walk you to your door?"

I shrug. "Aren't you old-fashioned?"

Something dark flashes across his face and I get the feeling that maybe I shouldn't have said that. I head up the pathway to my door and pause.

"This you? Number two?"

"Are you going to stalk me?" I ask and he barks out a laugh.

"I'm hoping you'll just agree to dinner with me so we can avoid that."

I decide he's damn adorable and let my bag slide down my arm. "I told you-- I don't have a lot of free time. I have to focus, or I won't be accepted into a company."

"How does that work?" he asks and leans a broad shoulder against the doorframe.

"I have to audition. It's really competitive and a lot of the more prestigious companies require an invitation in order to even audition."

"So, as with anything, it's all who you know."

"Pretty much."

"How many auditions have you done?"

"Just a couple so far." *And, one already rejected me,* I think.

"Ever consider dancing for the American Ballet Company here in LA?"

Is he kidding? Next to the American Ballet Theatre in New York, they're one of the best, the crème de la crème, and any dancer would be honored to be a part of their company. "Uh, yeah. ABC is kind of a pipe dream, though."

"Why's that?"

"Because I don't have any connections there. Which means no invite to audition."

He eyes me for a long moment, almost sizing me up. "Are you good?" he finally asks.

"I'm really good," I say without hesitation, my voice full of confidence.

"Then, I'll recommend you to my friend over there."

My eyes widened. *Wait, what?* "You have a friend at ABC?"

"Lizette LaFleur. The-"

"Director," I finished. I can't believe this.

"I've known her for years. She's a sweetheart."

I literally have no words.

"Do you think that would help you get an audition with them?" he asks.

"Um, yeah. I mean, it sure couldn't hurt." I'm instantly suspicious of his motives. "Why would you do that for me? I'm a complete stranger."

"Why don't we discuss it over dinner tomorrow?" he suggests with a twinkle in those blue eyes.

"You *are* persistent," I say again. But this time I smile. If he can help me get a pointe shoe into the American Ballet Company, I may do more than just eat dinner with him. I would smother his handsome face with kisses and do a million pirouettes especially for him.

"And?"

"And, I'll have dinner with you."

Chapter Four: Chaz

The next morning, after working out and a quick shower, I sit on the back patio of my house in the Encino Hills and eat a bowl of fresh fruit. My neighborhood is full of large homes perched over Ventura Boulevard and even though it gets hotter here in the San Fernando Valley, I like it better than the congested tangle of Hollywood or the constant smell of people smoking marijuana over on the West Side. And, of course, I have a pool, so the heat really doesn't bother me that much. Besides, I grew up in New York, so I'm used to humidity and all kinds of crazy weather.

As I chew a strawberry, I think over my plan to use Taylor to help fix my image. It's perfect. I need her help and she need mine. By being seen with a much-younger, beautiful girl, people will not view me as an old man who can't handle starring in an action flick. Instead, they will think I've still got it. Because if I can keep up with a hot, young thing like her, I can do anything.

I also really like the idea that she has a life and goals of her own. She seems to have a strong work ethic and a good head on her shoulders. I don't have to worry about her just hanging around here all day, bored. Or, worse, bugging me to put her in one of my movies.

Actresses are the worst and, other than a quick fuck, they're good for nothing. From my experience, they're self-centred, selfish and only worried about their looks. Now, don't get me wrong. Everyone in this town can be a little vain. You must be when every television screen is high-definition, 80 inches or more and people can see every pore on an actor's face.

But, at the same time, I've known actresses who spend 90 percent of their time at the medispa getting laser treatments, peels, facials and injectables. Call me old-fashioned, but I think that's a little much.

When I remember Taylor's natural beauty, my heart thumps a little harder. Her long red hair is the color of fire with different tints that range from gold to orange to red depending on the lighting. She has bright blue eyes that seemed to peer into my soul and her tight, little body is on a whole other level. It's clear how strong and fit she is and that's really attractive to me.

If I didn't know any better, she would be the perfect girlfriend. Unfortunately, after my disaster of a marriage, I know that it's best to keep your heart out of it. Real relationships mean nothing but complications, arguments and hurt.

And that is why I'm going into this arrangement with my eyes open and our signatures on the dotted line. Speaking of which…

I grab my phone and pull up Langston's number. "Hey, Lang, I need you to do something for me."

"What's up?" he asks.

"As my lawyer, I expect this to remain confidential and between us."

"Hang on," he says. "Let me get into work-mode." I hear some rustling and imagine him going into his office. "Alright, Mr. Stone, what can I help you with today?"

"I need you to put a contract together for me."

"What kind of contract?"

I hesitate. I trust Langston won't tell the other guys and he's my lawyer so no point in being coy. "A relationship contract."

He pauses. "Relationship? Can you clarify that?"

"I want to enter into a strictly PR relationship with a woman for a specified amount of time. We'll pretend to get engaged at some point and after we achieve our individual objectives, we break it off and quietly go our separate ways. No harm, no foul."

For a moment, he doesn't say anything, and I know he must be surprised by what I'm asking. "By when you need this?" he asks, keeping his voice neutral.

This is why I love Lang so much. Always the consummate professional. "Tonight?"

I hear him stifle back a sigh. "Then I'm going to need to clarify some details further with you right now."

"Fire away."

Langston runs through what feels like a thousand questions and I answer every one with complete honesty. After he has all the information he needs, he tells me he will email the document over tonight. I thank him and then he switches from my lawyer to my friend.

"Why are you doing this, Charles?"

Any time someone calls me by my full name, I know they're serious. "Because as much as I hate to admit it, the studio is right about me getting older. I might feel like I'm still 29, but that doesn't count. I need to prove to everyone out there that I still have what it takes. I can get the hot, young girl, get the action role and stay on people's radar."

"I take it you have someone in mind to sign this?"

"Well, I'm going to pitch the idea to her tonight. We're both in a position to help each other out, so why the hell not? I'm not going to sit around and count my gray hairs as they come in, Lang. I'm going to fight it every step of the way and go after what I want."

"What actress do you have in mind?"

I clear my throat. "She's not an actress. Just a regular woman."

"You don't know any regular women," he reminds me.

"I met one last night."

"At the club?" He sounds baffled and then it slowly dawns on him who I am talking about. "Oh, shit, no. Please, tell me it isn't that dancer."

I feel a prick of annoyance. "What does it matter? Who cares? It's all just going to be fake, anyway."

"Because she's like just turned 21, Chaz."

"Yeah, exactly what I'm looking for. So, what?"

"So, she's not in the industry and has no idea how vicious it can be. They're going to chew her up and spit her out."

"I disagree. I think people are going to adore her."

"She's going to get hurt."

"I won't let her get hurt."

But it's like he doesn't even hear me. "And, to pull this off, she's going to have to be able to put on one helluva performance."

"Thanks a lot, asshole."

"That's not what I mean. What I'm saying is maybe it would be best for you to choose an actress."

"No. I want Taylor and I know she's the right choice." Langston may as well quit talking because once I make up my mind, forget it. There's no changing it.

"Does she have any idea what you're about to hit her with tonight?"

"No," I admit. "But I can help her get a job she really wants, Lang. After I dangle the bait, she'll bite. No doubt about it."

Langston sighs long and hard. "Alright, pal. I hope you know what you're doing."

"I do. Don't even worry about it. Just get me that contract."

After we hang up, I decide that I need to wine and dine Taylor somewhere fancy tonight. I imagine as a student on a budget, she doesn't go to many expensive, 5-star restaurants, but I don't want to take her somewhere she won't like. I need to impress her and show her what life with me would be like. I have no idea what kind of food she likes or dislikes, so I send her a text: *Hey, Twinkle Toes-- what's your favorite food? I want to take you somewhere you will eat. No ordering just a salad.*

I have a few places in mind, but if she's a vegetarian or vegan then I can forget them. While I wait for her response, I look out over my yard and the view beyond. It's pretty spectacular, especially at night when the whole Valley lights up and it looks like a million sparkling fairies. When my phone beeps, I open it to see her text: *But I like salads. I also like chicken, fries, broccoli, mac and cheese and any kind of dessert lol. Oh, and yummy, sweet alcoholic drinks.*

Perfect. I'm taking her to The Penthouse at Mastro's in Beverly Hills. I tell her that I'll pick her up at six and to dress up. Then, I think about how I'm going to bring up my offer. It should prove to be a very tempting proposition and I expect her to agree.

Little do I know; Taylor isn't the type of person who does anything without thinking it through thoroughly first.

Chapter Five: Taylor

I spend more time getting ready for tonight than I ever have for a date before. Since he's an actor, I know he's used to being around gorgeous women who always look perfect and that's intimidating. I am definitely not anywhere close to perfect, so I make sure my hair and makeup look as good as it can. He said to dress up and since I rarely do, I actually have some clean clothes available. Damn, I really need to do laundry tomorrow.

I choose a cute baby doll dress and wedges. It's nice being able to put a dress on since all I ever wear are warm-ups, leotards, tights, off-the-shoulder sweatshirts, leggings, wrap shirts and tops and, of course, leg warmers.

But that's the life and wardrobe of a ballerina.

At six o'clock, there's a knock on my door and I open it to see Chaz. *Wow.* My stomach gives a little flutter and he's even better looking than I remember. He wears an expensive-looking charcoal suit with a blue tie that makes the color of his eyes pop. Cleanly-shaven and tan, he gives me a bright-white smile. "Ready?" he asks.

I nod and grab my purse. We head down the walkway, past the pool and bump into Ryan Fox, the owner and manager of Sunset Terrace. He's carrying a bag of food and probably just picked up dinner for him and Hailey.

"Hi, Taylor," he says and eyes Chaz. I think I see recognition pass through his green gaze.

"Hi. This is, uh, Chaz. Chaz, this is Ryan, my landlord."

"Nice to meet you," Chaz says.

Ryan gives a nod but looks suspicious. "You, too." Ryan watches out for all the girls here and when anyone brings a man around, he makes it known that he's here if we need him. Being former military special ops, he can be a bit intimidating.

"See you later," I say and keep walking.

"He lives here?" Chaz asks and glances over his shoulder at Ryan's receding figure.

"Yeah. With Hailey, his girlfriend."

That seems to make him relax and Chaz leads me over to a silver Mercedes. It's pretty fancy-looking, but I don't act like I'm impressed. After I get in, he shuts the door and walks around to the driver's side.

"So, where are we going?" I ask.

He glances over his shoulder and then pulls forward into traffic. "Thought I'd take you to Mastro's in Beverly Hills. Ever been there?"

I shake my head. "I don't usually get wine and dine offered by famous actors."

He grins. "Well, get used to it, Sugar Plum."

I can't help but laugh. "I danced that role last year. It was a dream come true and something I'd always aspired to since I was a little girl."

"Really? Was it difficult?"

"I had to perform a challenging pas de deux filled with bravura lifts. It's very intricate and tests your technique and stamina, but it looks so light and delicate. It's a beautiful solo. But, yeah, it was hard."

We stop at a light, and he looks over at me, blue eyes darkening. "I'd love to see your ballet dancing sometime."

I feel a strange pull to him and force myself to look back out the windshield, striving to keep things light. "I dance every day. Just swing on by."

"I'll have to take you up on that offer."

His low words make my stomach flip-flop.

When we pull up to the valet at Mastro's, I can tell this place is no joke and only caters to the hoity-toity in Los Angeles. *Definitely not my scene*, I think and feel my nerves kick up. The car door opens, and I step out and straighten my dress. Chaz walks up next to me and places a hand at my back, guiding me into the restaurant.

"Good evening, Mr. Stone," the hostess says with a bright smile. "You'll be dining in the Penthouse tonight, correct?"

"That's right," he says.

"Wonderful." She escorts us over to an elevator and hits the up button. While we wait for it, she stays with us. "I just loved your last film," she gushes.

"Thank you," Chaz says.

"Do you have any new projects in the works? Anything I should be on the lookout for?" she asks with a twinkle in her eye.

"I definitely have something new in the works," he says and glances at me.

"Good to know."

The door slides open, and we step inside while Miss Flirtatious Hostess hits the button for the top floor. "Enjoy your evening," she says and the door shuts.

Wow. I glance over at him, and he seems completely unfazed. Apparently, this must happen all the time. "Does everyone kiss your ass like that?" I ask and he barks out a laugh.

"Not everyone," he admits. "Mostly just the people who don't know me very well. Or the ones who want something."

"Hmm."

"What's that mean?" he asks in a flirty voice.

I shrug a shoulder. "It's just kind of weird."

He leans closer. "It's very weird," he agrees sotto voce and then gives me a devastating smile.

God, he has that megawatt movie star smile down pat, and butterflies take flight in my stomach again.

The elevator reaches the top floor, and we step out in the Penthouse part of the restaurant. *Fancy-shmancy,* I think, and look around. A hostess immediately walks over.

"Mr. Stone, so nice to see you again. Follow me to your table."

She guides us outside and everyone we pass seems to look over at us and I've never felt so self-conscious in my life. It's a gorgeous setup with fresh orchids on every table, fluffy pillows and gray and white decor.

Chaz motions for me to have a seat on the bench that runs along the edge of the building, covered in throw pillows. I sit down and spin around to see the top of a palm tree right behind me. I scoot up on my knees and glance over the side.

"Careful," he says.

I turn back around and sit down. "What? You think I'm going to fall?"

A strange look passes over his face.

"I have a very good balance," I inform him.

"I'm sure you do," he says.

He studies me intently for a moment and I feel my cheeks heat up. *Oh, no.* My face is going to turn as red as my hair. I take a sip of water and look around, hoping for a cool breeze to help my flushed face.

"You have an adorable blush," he says.

I cover my face and want to die of embarrassment. "Please, don't talk about it. You'll only make it worse."

He chuckles and a server comes over and tells us the specials. When he asks for our drink orders, Chaz requests a fancy-sounding bourbon and then looks at me. "Something sweet, right?"

I nod, not sure what to order. I have a feeling my usual vodka sour will earn me a sour look from the snooty waiter.

"How about a salty caramel martini?" Chaz suggests.

"Ooh, okay. That sounds delish."

We both look over the menu and I decide on getting all the favorites I had mentioned to him in my earlier text. Of course, he orders some expensive steak.

While we wait for our food, I suck the salty caramel martini down in record time. "This is delicious," I say, and he instantly orders me another. When round two arrives, I take a sip and study him over the rim of my salt-covered glass. "Can I ask you something?"

"Anything," he says and leans forward.

"Why did you ask me out?"

"What man in his right mind wouldn't want a chance to spend more time with you?"

"That sounds like a line out of a movie," I tell him.

"It's true, though. You're beautiful, smart and talented."

"I'm also a nobody. Why aren't you with some famous actress?"

"Because it's not all it's cracked up to be," he says in a jaded voice. As he takes a long sip of his bourbon whiskey, I watch the muscles in his tan throat work and decide that everything about this man so far is attractive. And, for me, that's dangerous because he could potentially distract me from my goals.

"I also have another reason," he admits. "But we can discuss that later."

My curiosity is piqued. "You can't just drop that on me and not expect me to ask any questions. Now I have to know."

"Later."

"Now."

He shakes his burnished-blond head and smirks. "Sorry, TuTu. That conversation will have to take place somewhere much more private than this."

As if to prove his point, a woman stops at our table and starts gushing over him and then begs for a selfie and an autograph. He complies, the perfect gentleman, and she leaves with stars in her eyes.

"I take it that happens a lot?"

"Yes and no," he tells me. "Depends on where I am."

"Does it bother you?"

He shrugs. "It's a part of the job so I try to take it with a grain of salt."

"What's the craziest place a fan approached you?" I ask.

Chaz swirls his drink then meets my gaze. "It was kind of embarrassing."

"Tell me." I lean forward, excited to hear.

He lets out a sigh. "Well, let me preface this by saying I have never been so sick as I was a few years ago when I got food poisoning."

I cringe.

"You still want to hear this?"

I nod in anticipation.

"So, I just finished filming and was at the airport, literally dying in a bathroom stall. I couldn't stop puking and...whatever else...and someone knocked on the door and wanted a photo."

"Oh, my God, you poor thing."

"It was humiliating, and I think I was a bit delirious at that point."

"What did you do?"

"I said I was a little busy and I think she got the picture because she eventually left."

"*She?* So, a woman followed you into the men's bathroom?" I ask in disbelief.

"Yeah."

"That's insane," I say and look up as the server sets our dinners in front of us. The bowl of gorgonzola macaroni and cheese looks much better than my frozen dinner the other night and I can't wait to try it. I also have a steaming side of broccoli florets and french-fried potatoes. I murmur a thank you and look over at the thick Porterhouse steak Chaz ordered which was $70.

"You eat a lot of steak?" I ask.

"Nope. But I do treat myself occasionally."

Dinner is delicious and I find myself enjoying Chaz's company. A lot. It's been so long since a man paid any attention to me and he's pouring it on me. I decline more alcohol because two martinis have me buzzing and I need to keep a somewhat clear head.

Especially when Chaz asks me to go back to his place with him.

"So, we can discuss my...proposition," he clarifies.

Instantly wary, I wonder what he wants from me. I have nothing to offer so I'm a little nervous. Does he think I'm going to sleep with him because that is not going to happen? I decide to be upfront and just let him know how I feel. "First of all, I'm not comfortable going to your house since I barely know you. And, secondly, if you think I'm going to fall into bed with you, you're wrong."

"If it puts your mind at ease, I have no intention of seducing you tonight, Taylor. I just want to talk about business."

"Business?"

"I have a proposition for you and, trust me, you'll be interested."

"How can you be so sure?"

"Let's just say it's mutually-beneficial. Will you come hear me out?"

I am beyond intrigued. What could he possibly want from me? And what could I have to gain from him? "Can we go somewhere more public?" The moment the words leave my mouth, a couple of girls approach the table and ask for a picture.

After they leave, he lifts a brow. "This is an extremely private matter, and we'd get interrupted."

As he signs the bill, I think about it. I'm not overly concerned that he would do anything to hurt me. And the fact that he's famous means he should be on his best behavior because if he tried anything creepy, I'd spread that shit all over social media so fast his head would spin from all my hashtags.

"Well?" he asks as we head over to the elevator.

"I'm thinking," I say.

Down on the street, as we wait for the valet to get his car, cameras start flashing. It's strange and I turn away. It's not like they want pictures of me, anyway.

Chaz moves up beside me and blocks me from the paparazzi. "You, okay?" he asks.

I can hear the concern in his voice. It's actually kind of sweet. "Yeah, thanks."

He reaches out, takes my hand and squeezes it. "Just ignore them."

I look up into his cobalt blue eyes and suddenly feel extremely special. When the valet returns, Chaz tips him and we get into the car. He looks over at me, waiting for my decision.

"Okay, I'll go hear your mysterious proposition. But just so you know, I have mace in my purse and I'm not afraid to use it."

"I have to say I'm glad to hear that since I know you sometimes walk home at 2am."

His dry tone makes me smile and about 25 minutes later, his Mercedes heads up into a neighborhood of Encino Hills. The houses are huge, and I can't help but press my face to the window and watch as we pass. At the end of a quiet cul-de-sac, he pulls up a driveway and into a three-car garage.

I get out and follow him inside. *Holy crap.* The place is amazing, and for the first time, it really dawns on me that I'm in the company of a true movie star. He must be worth millions. I pick my jaw up off the ground, trying not to gawk at everything. It's so well-put together and I assume he had a designer choose the decor. The artwork, vases of fresh flowers and clean, modern look of it all feels very inviting.

I follow him to an elegant dining room table, and he pulls a chair out for me. "Have a seat." I notice a stack of papers in front of his chair as I sit down, and my mind is going crazy wondering what this is all about.

"I think we're in a position to help each other and I want you to listen carefully before you make a decision. Okay?"

"Okay." I lean forward, curiosity eating away at me.

Chapter Six: Chaz

I am all-business as I fold my hands and lay them on top of the contract. "The gist of it is this: we enter into a fake, whirlwind romance where you pretend to be my new girlfriend for a certain amount of time. We'll get engaged at some point and, in return, I will secure you an audition invitation to the American Ballet Company."

Taylor's bright blue eyes widen, and I keep going.

"After we achieve our goals, we quietly break off the engagement and go our separate ways." She just blinks and I can tell she doesn't know what to say so I give her a moment to process it. *Yep, I've made her speechless.* "Well?"

"Well, that's a lot to think about," she says slowly. "Is that a contract?" She nods to the stack of papers beneath my hands.

"Yes, and I'll be more than happy to go through it with you, page by page. I want you to feel completely comfortable with our arrangement."

Taylor opens her mouth then immediately closes it. I can practically hear her thoughts, spinning in her head. "First of all, why in the world do you need a fake girlfriend? After being out with you tonight, I think pretty much any woman would like that title."

"Maybe, but I want to avoid all the drama that comes along with a real relationship. I want to keep living my life and not have to worry about calling, texting, explaining, fighting and all the other bullshit. I want someone on my arm to go to events with me, smile pretty for the camera and help mend my image."

"You want a trophy girlfriend."

"Yes, that's pretty much it."

For a moment, she looks a bit offended. "What's wrong with your image?"

I shift in my chair. "Lately, I've been hearing some negative comments about me getting older."

"You're 42, not 72."

"That's what I said!" I exclaim and can't help but crack a smile. I like that we're on the same wavelength. "But, in my business, 30 is considered old. There's a role I want, and the studio doesn't think I can pull it off. They're eyeing someone younger and it's pissing me off."

"So, you think that by dating a younger woman then people will view you as young again."

"Exactly."

"Hmm."

"What're you thinking?" I ask. I realize I'm on the edge of my seat and I really want her to agree. But I can't exactly figure out what she's thinking.

"I'm a little shocked, to be honest."

"Don't you want a chance to get into ABC?"

"Of course, I do."

"So, what's the big deal? You go to some parties and be seen in public with me and then go to your big audition."

Her face flushes. "It's not that easy. I have some questions and concerns."

I push the contract over to her. "Take a look and ask away."

Taylor begins to flip through the pages, reading through the clauses. "I guess I'm wondering about, um, the physical stuff…"

"Sex?"

My directness seems to fluster her, and her cheeks turn a deep shade of crimson. "Among other things, yes."

She doesn't make eye contact and stares down at a page, curling the edge with her finger.

"Page eight," I say, all business-like.

Taylor chews on her lower lip, flips to page eight and begins to read. I notice her shoulders relax a bit.

"We're not going to sleep together," I clarify. "This will be a strictly-business relationship." She instantly looks relieved, and I can't help but feel a little miffed. Would having sex with me be that big of a chore for her?

"And this part here about public displays of affection?"

"Required and non-negotiable."

"And that includes what exactly?"

"Holding hands, kissing, staring deeply into each other's eyes and acting like we're so in love that nothing else exists."

"Well, that clarifies it." She flips another page. "How big of a time-commitment will all this be? I have dance class all day and work at night. I'm just not sure how to fit you into my busy schedule."

Her busy schedule... I can't help but smile again. "You can keep attending your classes, but you're going to have to stop dancing at that club."

A frown creases her forehead. "That club pays my bills."

"I'll pay your bills."

"What?"

"Page 11."

She skips ahead and reads the clause that outlines a weekly stipend to cover all her expenses. When her brows raise in surprise, I'm guessing she got to the part that promises her $2,000 a week.

"Two grand? *A week?*"

"I thought the figure seemed fair."

"Um, yeah, I'd say." For a long moment, she studies me. "Just how rich are you?"

I burst out laughing. "You don't mince words do you?"

"Well, that would definitely pay my bills. And allow me to focus completely on ballet."

"And me."

"Right. And you." She gives me a speculative look. "Why *me?*"

"Why not?"

"You're avoiding my question."

I sigh. *Am I attracted to her?* Yes, of course. *Can I tell her that?* No, absolutely not. "Because you have a youthful exuberance and a zest for life that's contagious. I felt it the moment I saw you at Club Noir. Your energy draws people to you and that's what I need. If everyone loves you then they'll love me again." *Shit, I sound sad and needy*, I think.

"I don't suppose it had anything to do with the fact that I was dancing in a cage, did it?"

"You're a smart ass."

"I know," she says and tosses her long, red hair over a shoulder.

"An unapologetic smart ass."

I watch her skim over the last few pages and then look up at me. "I'm going to have to read through this thoroughly before I make my final decision. I also will most likely have some additions and corrections. Does that work for you?"

Unbelievable. "I don't suppose I have a choice in the matter."

"You're asking a lot."

"I'm giving a lot, too."

When she starts toying with the edge of the pages again, I frown. "What are you concerned about?"

"I know you said things will remain strictly professional behind closed doors…"

"That's right."

"But I just need some clarification."

"Okay." I sit back and cross my arms over my chest. "Basically, I expect you to help improve my image by being the perfect girlfriend which means you're at my side, supportive and always looking nice. Be your charming self. You'll accompany me everywhere in public-- work events, dates, premieres. I want to create photo ops and for everyone to wonder who you are and then fall in love with you. I do expect public displays of affection, but behind closed doors, it's a business relationship. You're going to need to be able to turn it on and off. Think of me more like a Daddy figure. I'll make sure you're taken care of while we're together. I'm very generous, Taylor."

I know the temptation to accept my deal is high. Taylor has a feisty side which makes me believe she's competitive and would probably do just about anything to get into a prestigious ballet company. And, here I am, offering it to her on a silver platter.

"And you'll make sure I get invited to audition at ABC?"

"Yes."

She lets out a breath. "Well, I have a lot to think about."

"I'm going to need an answer by tomorrow."

"Then, I should probably get home and start reading through this contract."

"C'mon, I'll drive you home," I tell her.

When I pull the Mercedes up to the curb in front of the Sunset Terrace sign, Taylor unbuckles her seatbelt and turns to face me. "Thank you for the dinner."

"You're welcome."

"I'll, ah, let you know my decision in the morning."

I nod and then reach for my door handle.

"It's okay, you don't have to walk me up. I just saw some of my neighbors and they'll just be nosey."

"Are you sure?"

"Yeah, thanks, though."

I watch her open the door and slide out.

"Taylor?"

She turns and peers back into the car. "Huh?"

"I didn't make you sign a Non-Disclosure Agreement when I probably should have, so please keep our conversation confidential."

"And, what're you going to do if I don't? Sue me?" she asks, a twinkle in her blue eyes. "Good luck with that, Mr. Stone. I don't even have enough quarters to do my laundry."

Then, she gives me a dazzling smile, a little wave and shuts the door. I shake my head and watch her saunter off. Halfway up the pathway, she does a little ballet spin that makes me smile.

Chapter Seven: Taylor

After my evening with Chaz, I sit down on my bed and scour through the contract with a fine-tooth comb. There's nothing surprising and he's not trying to pull a fast one on me. Everything in it, he talked about and addressed to some degree.

All I must do is pretend to be his girlfriend and then his fiancée. He's going to pay me $2,000 a week! I've never had that much money in my life, and I plan to save it. If we're together for two months, I'll have $16,000 and that's insane to me.

And, for what? Going to fancy restaurants and parties? Dressing up and attending Industry events on his arm? I have a feeling that quite a few girls would kill to be in my position.

Still, though, a part of me is nervous and a little unsure.

Okay, a bit unsure.

I pour over the contract for the tenth time and weigh my options. And the more I think about it, the more I realize that accepting it is the best thing that I can do for my career. Because let's face it, ABC is not knocking on my door any time soon and I would die for an audition invitation.

I think the part that makes me most nervous is Chaz himself. He's extremely good-looking and he said that I need to be able to turn my performance on and off. But, what if I can't? What if I make the horrendous mistake of developing feelings for him?

No. I can't let that happen. He made it quite clear that he needs a woman who will agree to keep things professional. So, I'll just have to ignore his movie star looks, wit and charm. I'll pretend his eyes don't look quite so blue or that his burnished hair isn't tempting me to run my fingers through it. Maybe he wears lifts and when he takes his shoes off, he loses a few inches, and he isn't as tall as he seems. And maybe he had really bad breath and I won't want to get too close.

Yeah, right. His breath smelled like peppermint toothpaste and the soles of his shoes didn't give him any extra inches. He's just naturally a perfect 6'2".

But the one thing I don't think I'll be able to control is the way my stomach drops every time I'm around him.

Sleep doesn't come easy for me, and I toss and turn all night, consumed with thoughts of Chaz and the contract. Luckily, it's the weekend and I don't have dance classes so I can sleep in a little bit. After a rough night's sleep, I crawl out of bed, wander into the bathroom and have to practically climb over the mountain of dirty laundry. It's getting ridiculous now and I must do something about it soon. Maybe tomorrow, I think.

Maybe.

After a quick shower, I pour some orange juice into a glass and realize that I didn't check the mail yesterday. I still haven't heard from my San Diego audition, and I decide to go look. When I open the door, I practically trip over a large mason jar. "What the hell?"

I stoop down and realize it's full of quarters. It weighs a ton and I lug it into my apartment, pulling off the attached note. "Do your laundry, Dancing Queen. C."

My traitorous heart does a somersault. There must be like $200 worth of quarters in here and enough to help me do my laundry for months. *Well, that was sweet of him.* And the thoughtful gesture makes me feel good until I go down to my mailbox and find a rejection letter from San Diego Ballet.

"Fuck," I hiss. I read through it, and it says the same crap that my other rejection letter said. I don't understand. I did well at both auditions. I remind myself how subjective the whole process is, but it's not helping. A part of me just wants to break down and cry. Suddenly, I feel extremely defeated.

"Hey, Tay. What's wrong?"

I look up and see my neighbor Jasmine.

"Oh, you know. Just getting rejected right and left."

"Aww, honey, I'm sorry." She throws an arm around my shoulders. "Why don't you come over and I'll make some chocolate chip pancakes to cheer you up?"

I start walking to her place, feeling like the biggest, most untalented loser, and it's going to take more than pancakes to turn my day around.

"Thanks, Jazz," I say. I realize I sound so glum, and she must hear it, too.

"Is it something else that's bothering you?" she asks as we head into her apartment. Jasmine is 25 and the oldest of the girls here in our group. Besides being extremely beautiful, she's smart and very perceptive when it comes to other people's lives. She also has way more life experience and loves to dole out advice.

I nod and sit down at the small kitchen table. She starts gathering bowls and ingredients to make the pancakes. "Spill it," she says.

"Actually, I could really use some advice."

"That's my specialty."

I watch her dump some pancake mixture into a bowl along with an egg and some oil. Then, she starts to mix it all up, brow raised, waiting for me to tell her what's bothering me. Chaz told me not to say anything, but Jasmine won't tell anyone. I don't think so, anyway. "You can't tell anyone, though," I say. "You have to promise."

She stops stirring, brown eyes sparkling. "Ooh, a secret? My lips are sealed."

"Do you know who Chaz Stone is?"

"The actor?" she asks, and I nod. "Of course! He's totally hot."

"Well, he sorts of came to Club Noir a couple of nights ago and, um, asked me out."

"*What*?" she screams. She drops the spatula in the bowl and batter splatters.

"Yeah, and that's not even the most interesting part." I pause, not sure how to tell her that a movie star wants me to be his fake girlfriend. "So, apparently, he's been getting some slack for getting older and he thinks that by having a younger woman on his arm he can regain his youthful image."

"Oh, my God! He wants you to be his girlfriend, doesn't he?"

"Yes and no. He wants me to be his *fake* girlfriend."

"Fake?"

"He wants a PR relationship, not a real one."

"What's in it for you?"

"An audition at ABC."

"Oh, shit," she says and sinks down into a chair.

"Exactly."

"So, you'd have to sign a contract?"

I nod. "He already wrote it up. I have it next door and I've read through it like 100 times. But I'm so confused."

"What are you confused about?"

"Everything," I admit. "I got rejected from both ballet companies I auditioned for and now I'm wondering if I'm just not good enough."

"You are an amazing dancer!"

"I used to think so, but maybe I'm not as good as I thought."

"No, you're ridiculously talented, Taylor. If those companies didn't want you, it's their loss and not meant to be."

"But, if I couldn't make the cut for San Francisco and San Diego, why would ABC want me? They're the best of the best."

"It's all who you know in this town. You know that. Do you think I'd be walking runways all over the world if I'd never met Lukas? He launched my career."

"But you're so good."

"Talent will only take you so far. Then, you have to be smart and meet someone who believes in you."

"Chaz told me he's good friends with the director over there-- Lizette LeFleur."

"That's what you need. An in. I bet the dancers who were chosen over you knew someone at those companies. I highly doubt they were more talented. You work harder than anybody I know, and you deserve a shot over at ABC."

"Thanks, Jazz. That means a lot."

"So, I think we should eat some chocolate chip pancakes and go over that contract." She gives me a devilish smile and I chuckle.

"Let's do it."

Twenty minutes later, I douse my pancakes in syrup and watch as Jasmine starts to read through the contract. She asks me a couple of things here and there and when she finishes it, she looks up, her dark eyes glowing.

"This is too exciting. I feel like I should call TMZ."

"Jazz! You can't say a word to anyone!"

"I know, I know. I'm just kidding. Although, I think they do pay for stories and this one's a doozy."

"I need your advice, please."

"My advice is to sign at the dotted line before he decides to ask someone else because you're taking too long to make a decision."

"Really?"

"It's a win-win situation. He can reclaim his younger, hot status by being seen around town with you. And you can get into ABC. It's perfect. And, let's be honest, if Chaz Stone were a Skittle, I'd be wanting to taste that rainbow all night long."

I burst out laughing. "Oh, my God."

"Looking at him will hardly be a chore for the next couple of months."

"That's kind of what I'm scared of."

"What do you mean?"

"He's really attractive and charming. What if I start to fall for him?"

"You can't. It can only be a business arrangement, so you have to go into it with your eyes wide open."

"Right," I say.

She eyes me for a moment. "If you feel yourself getting too close, you have to nip it in the bud. Collect your money, secure your audition and, most importantly, keep your thoughts clean and above the belt, my little virgin." She gives me a funny look. "Does he know?"

"God, no! How embarrassing."

"I wonder what he would think if he knew?"

"He'd probably wonder what was wrong with me."

"Hmm, I seriously doubt that."

"You think he'd like it?

"He's older, jaded and divorced. I bet he'd fucking love it."

"Really?"

"Yeah, so you probably shouldn't tell him. Unless y'all decide to cross that line and put the wand in the chamber of secrets." She winks at me, and I feel a blush creep up my face.

"Where do you come up with these sayings?"

Jasmine laughs. "Seriously, though, Tay. You can't stay a virgin forever and what a way to lose it. With a GD celebrity!"

"You are really too much," I tell her.

"What can I say? The older men are snatching up all our Sunset Terrace virgins-- first Savannah, then Hailey, now you. My little girls are all becoming women. I feel like such a proud momma."

"You're crazy!" I can't help but laugh.

After we settle down, she finishes her last bite of pancake. "He's pretty upfront and clear, though, that there will be no sexual relations between the two of you. Do you think he's gay?"

"No, I don't get that impression at all. I think he just wants me to be comfortable with the arrangement and know there won't be any expectations to sleep with him. And I really appreciate that."

"Hmm."

"What's that mean?"

"It means, we'll see."

Yes, I guess we shall see because I'm about to tell Chaz Stone that he has a deal. I'm going to be his new, fake girlfriend/fiancée. A little shiver of anticipation runs through me.

Chapter Eight: Chaz

The more time that passes, the more nervous I get. I'm on fucking pins and needles by the time I see Taylor's text pop up late that afternoon. I swipe the bar over and read her message: *Before I agree, can we add a couple of things to the contract?*

I wonder what she wants to add. I have a movie premiere to attend tonight, and I wanted her by my side. *Can you come over now?* I text back. I don't mean to rush her, but once I get something in my head, I'm ready to roll. My little ballerina sure likes to overthink things.

Okay, on my way, she responds.

Great. I just want to wrap this up and move forward.

When Taylor arrives, we sit down at the dining room table again and I can't help but think how adorable she looks with her hair up on her head in a messy bun and wearing a tank top and shorts.

"Thanks for the quarters," she says. "They will be put to good use. One of these days."

"You're welcome," I tell her. "Now, what did you want to add?"

She sits up straighter. "You mentioned I can continue my dance classes and I want to make sure that's written in here somewhere. Specifically, that they are Monday through Friday from 9am to 4pm. And, if I'm in a performance, I will also have rehearsals."

"Do you have a show coming up?"

"No, but I just want to be covered. Just in case."

I nod and jot it down in the margin for Langston to add. "Anything else?"

"Yes."

I notice her cheeks turning pink and I force myself to keep a straight face. Obviously, she has something to say about the sex clause. I've never known anyone to blush so furiously, and I love it.

"I just want to emphasize that you do not cross any lines when it comes to sex because that is something that I am waiting to experience with someone who I am in a real relationship with."

As her words sink in, I meet her blue gaze and realize she's telling me that she's a virgin. I guess a part of me is surprised by her revelation, but another part isn't because I understand what it means to dedicate your life to a profession-- relationships inevitably move to the back burner. "You're still a virgin?"

"Yes."

"I understand and like I said before, behind closed doors, it's all business."

She lets out a breath and nods. "Okay, then I guess I'm ready to sign."

I slide a pen across the table and watch closely as she scrawls her name on the last page and dates it. Then, I pull it back over and sign my name. *Done deal, baby.* I feel a wave of relief wash through me and I can't wait to get this farce of a show on the road.

Then, I stand up and offer my hand. "I'll have my lawyer add your clause. I look forward to doing business with you, Miss Quinn."

When she stands and accepts my hand, I can't ignore the electricity that zings between us. But I have to ignore it, so I force myself to let go of her small hand and keep my voice level and professional when I say, "I have an event tonight and I'm going to need you there."

"Tonight?"

"That's right. My stylist will be here in-" I glance down at the large platinum watch on my wrist, "-ten minutes and she will help you get ready."

"Um, okay."

"Do you want anything to drink or-"

"Hey, bro," Brandon interrupts and walks into the room. "Did you know-" He abruptly stops speaking when he sees Taylor and does a double-take.

Talk about timing, I think. Ah, well, Brand would've met her sooner than later, anyway. "Taylor, this is my brother, Brandon. He hangs out here more than he should. Brand, meet Taylor Quinn."

Brand's mouth lifts in a knowing smirk and I feel the urge to punch him. "Nice to meet you, Taylor. And the reason I'm here so much is because if I didn't take care of half the shit going on in this guy's life, he'd be lost."

When she smiles at him, I feel a prick of jealousy. An emotion I haven't felt in years. Hell, maybe ever. "I need to talk to you," I tell my brother and start walking toward the kitchen.

Brand tosses Taylor a charming smile and right before we are out of the room, he leans closer and hits my shoulder. "Are you about to win that bet?"

"Shut it," I growl. Once we're out of her earshot, I turn to Brand. "Just so you know what's going on, Taylor and I just signed this." I toss the contract on the counter.

Brand arches a brow and reaches for the contract. He begins to flip through it and his jaw drops. "A fake relationship? Are you insane?"

"Lower your voice," I snap. "Christ, you're gonna scare her off before we even get started."

"Why're you doing this? Because of what Cal said?"

"C'mon, Brand. I'm not ready to play any kind of grandfather and if that means being seen around town with some hot, young thing on my arm then fine."

My brother lets out a groan. "I hope you know what you're doing."

"It's a business relationship, that's all. But no one can know."

"I'm assuming Lang knows because he drew this up, right?"

I nod. "Him, you, me and Taylor. Only the four of us know and I'd like to keep it that way."

"I wish you would've talked to me about this first."

"There's nothing to discuss. I'm taking measures to save my image."

"I understand that, but what about her?"

I have no idea what he means. "What about her? She's getting compensated."

"That's not what I mean. She seems like a nice girl-- and innocent and naive. Did it ever occur to you that you might be taking advantage?"

"No. This is a mutually-beneficial arrangement."

"Okay. If you say so."

I frown, not liking that he thinks I'm some kind of predator or something. Actually, it really pisses me off. "I am taking care of her."

"That's kind of what I'm afraid of, Chaz."

"What the hell does that mean?"

"Here's my prediction. That girl is going to suddenly find herself in the middle of this fairy tale, Cinderella-fucking story, fall in love with the movie star and then wake up alone and back in rags. And, most likely debauched."

I grit my jaw. "I've been very clear how this will end. And, what the hell, Brand? You don't think I have any self-control? Jesus, give me some credit."

Brand just shakes his head. "She's young, Chaz. You will be able to walk away when it's over, but will she?"

"She knows exactly what she's getting into," I insist.

"I hope so."

I don't like that he's trying to burst my bubble. "Why don't you go pick up my dry cleaning or something?"

"Fuck you."

"I'm not going to hurt her, so you just relax. I don't know why you care so much, anyway."

"I won't say another word about it."

For a moment, I glare at the black and white tiled floor. Then, the doorbell rings. "That's Marta," I say.

"Taylor going to the premiere with you tonight?"

"Of course."

He nods. "Well, I hope you get what you want out of this whole thing. You know I'm always on your side."

His words make me relax a little. "Thanks, Brand."

He nods.

A few minutes later, I introduce Taylor to Marta, my stylist, and she quickly takes over. "I'm putting you in the navy Gucci tonight, Chaz, so I've brought some complimentary options for Miss Quinn."

"Oh, please, just call me Taylor," she says with a little laugh.

It's obvious she's not used to being fawned over and I'm glad to be the one to change that. Taylor is beautiful and should have access to the finest things and I'm going to make sure of it. At least, for the next couple of months.

Marta whisks her off to one of the guest bedrooms. Luckily, she's also a former makeup artist so I know Taylor is in good hands. Honestly, though, she doesn't need much done. Taylor Quinn could walk into the premiere tonight with no makeup and wearing a simple sundress and steal the show.

I have a feeling she's going to cause quite a raucous tonight, and I look forward to shaking things up a bit. The guest list will be a Who's Who in Hollywood and I hope I see some friendly faces. In the meantime, though, I need to go take a shower and get ready myself. We don't have that much time and it's important that we impress everyone tonight.

After all, it's going to be our big debut as a couple and the first time I introduce Taylor to the world. The more I think about it, the more excited I get. I couldn't have chosen a better woman to do this, and I can't wait to show her off on the red carpet.

I just hope she doesn't get nervous or freak out. If you're not used to all the attention, it can be a little nerve-wracking. People calling your name, snapping your picture, shoving lights in your face...it definitely takes some skill getting used to, but I have faith in Taylor. She may not be an actress, but she is a performer.

I remember back to when I first saw her up in that cage at Club Noir. Yeah, she was definitely putting on a show. She was also having a lot of fun doing it and she mesmerized me. I have a feeling she's going to do the same thing again tonight and steal the spotlight.

It doesn't take me long to get ready and I don't need Marta to fawn all over me. Just Taylor. I've been doing this a long time and have it down to an art. So, when I step out of my master bedroom, dressed and ready, with ten minutes to spare before the car service arrives, I head down to the back family room and pop in to see what Brand is doing.

When I walk in, he hits pause on whatever show he's watching on the floor to ceiling TV screen. "Looking sharp, bro," he says.

I straighten my tie and nod. "Thanks," I mumble and swipe my hand over some lint on my jacket sleeve.

He eyes me and his sharp, blue-gray gaze narrows. "You seem nervous."

Do I? I'm never nervous, but I do feel a little on edge. "I'm fine."

"Uh-huh."

"You know, sometimes you can be a royal pain in my ass."

"That's what younger brothers do. You should know that by now."

Just when I'm about to make a sarcastic remark, Marta appears. Taylor walks in directly behind her and I strain to get a glimpse. When she steps into my line of vision, my heart thunders and my mouth go dry.

Holy. Shit.

She's beyond stunning in a strapless midnight blue party dress with a tulle skirt spun with silver threads. Her long red hair looks straight and silky and I have the urge to run my fingers through it. Her skin is so pale it practically glows, and she looks delicate and ethereal, like some kind of moon goddess.

I have a compliment for her, but the words get stuck in my throat so Brand gives a low whistle. "You'll be the belle of the ball," he says.

"Thank you," she murmurs.

I take a step closer, still trying to process how gorgeous she looks when she turns her attention to me and smiles.

"Marta here is an absolute genius. I'm not sure how she did it, but I feel like a Disney princess."

I hear Brand clear his throat, but I ignore him. "You look beautiful," I finally manage to say. "Are you ready?" When she nods, I place my hand at her back and guide her out.

"Have fun," Brand says with a sly smirk.

I lead Taylor out the front door and over to the black SUV that's waiting to take us to Grauman's Chinese Theatre in Hollywood. Once we're settled in the back seat, she looks over at me and smiles.

"This is crazy," she whispers and runs a nervous hand over her tulle skirt. "I feel just like Cinderella."

Brand's words ring through my ears, and I shift in my seat.

Here's my prediction. That girl is going to suddenly find herself in the middle of this fairy tale, Cinderella-fucking story, fall in love with the movie star and then wake up alone and back in rags. And, most likely debauched.

No. I reach over and give her hand a reassuring squeeze. I'm not going to mess around with this little girl's head. Or, her tempting, little body.

Absolutely-fucking-not, I tell myself.

Chapter Nine: Taylor

So far, this night feels unreal, and it hasn't even started yet. I truly feel like Cinderella on her way to the ball. I dress up for ballet performances, but this is totally different. While that feels more theatrical this feels magical. Like I'm stepping into some fantasy world where I've never been allowed to venture before.

When we arrive at the famous red and gold theatre, the SUV pulls up to the curb and Chaz looks over at me, blue eyes intense. "You ready?" he asks.

I look out my window and see a long red carpet, a ton of people and cameras flashing everywhere. It all looks so exciting, and I hope that I don't screw up and embarrass Chaz or myself. "I've never been to a movie premiere," I say.

"After tonight, you'll be a pro."

"We never discussed any details. Like how we met."

"Just smile and let me do the talking. Okay?"

I nod and take a deep breath as Chaz gets out and walks around to open my door. Then, he reaches out and I place my hand in his. He pulls me from the car, and it feels like I'm having an out of body experience.

Suddenly, everything becomes surreal as we make our way into the crush. People scream his name; flashes brighten the night and I feel like I'm watching myself from above as we meet his publicist Liz.

Liz gives him a panicked, who-the-hell-is-this look, but Chaz just smiles. "Relax, Lizzy."

"You could've given me a heads-up," she says and looks over at me. "You didn't mention a date."

"She's more than a date," Chaz says and squeezes my hand. "This is Taylor Quinn, my new girlfriend."

"Oh, Jesus. I'm gonna have a heart attack."

"You'll be fine," Chaz says and pats her shoulder. "You always are no matter what stunt I pull."

"I thought your stunt days were over. But, apparently not," she adds in a wry voice and shakes her head. "People are going to go insane. *Shit.* Okay, no more than two minutes per reporter. I'll keep scooting you along or we'll never get you inside."

Liz escorts us to the edge of the red carpet and I hear her whisper to Chaz through gritted teeth, "One of these days, I'm going to kill you."

"Never. You know you love me," he says and flashes that movie star smile of his.

With my hand held securely in his, Chaz and I step onto the carpet. It's extremely intimidating, but I do my best to smile and stay close to his side. We make our way over to the first reporter in line and she shoves a microphone in Chaz's face.

"Who is this gorgeous young woman on your arm?" she asks.

"This is Taylor," Chaz announces and squeezes my hand.

"Well, Taylor, you are absolutely glowing. Do I sense a romance brewing?"

When she turns the microphone to me, I freeze for a moment, not sure how I should respond. But Chaz did say he wants everyone to believe we're in the midst of a whirlwind romance. "Thank you," I say and smile. "But, if I'm glowing, it's only because I'm standing next to this amazing man."

I look up at Chaz and see the approval in his blue eyes. Liz hurries us along and everyone wants to know who I am. They are all so unbelievably nosey! It's overwhelming, but super-exciting and I'm not going to lie-- I love the attention and being on Chaz's arm makes me feel special.

I can't get over how handsome he looks. His cobalt blue eyes pop against the navy suit he wears and he's so very tall. I see how other women look at him and know he's definitely a hot commodity. But he pays them no attention. All his focus is on me.

By the time we reach the tenth reporter, I've gotten comfortable with the answers we've been giving and the playful banter we're exchanging. And then, I get thrown for a loop when the interviewer catches me off-guard.

"Good Lord," she exclaims and fans herself. "There's so much chemistry and heat pouring off the two of you! Let's see some of that sizzle up close, if you know what I mean."

What is she asking us to do exactly? I wonder. Before I can think too hard about it, Chaz turns me toward him. Something flashes in his gaze before he lowers his head and captures my mouth in a kiss that makes my blood heat and stomach flutter.

Holy freaking cow!

His lips move over mine and my mouth opens just a bit. All rational thought leaves my brain as I kiss him back, leaning into him and clutching his suit jacket in my hands. The kiss is perfect, not too long or short, and when he pulls back, I see blue lightning spark in his eyes.

People whistle and cheer while Liz scoots us forward. I know that was all just for show, but it didn't feel very fake. In fact, every cell in my body is still buzzing. *Keep it together, Tay.*

Ten minutes later, we finally finish the red carpet and stand in front of the theatre's huge front doors. Chaz smirks at Liz. "Told you everything would be fine," he says.

Liz glances at me and shakes her head. "That could've been disastrous. Thank God, you're a pro." She smiles at me. "Both of you."

"Are you staying for the movie?"

"Oh, hell, no. My other client is here somewhere, and I need to say goodbye and get home to my poor husband."

"Easton is here?" Chaz asks. "I'd like to say hello."

"Yes. Oh, there they are!" She waves to the actress and her husband.

Chaz lays a hand against my back and escorts me into the luxurious lobby and up to the hottest couple I have ever seen in my life. I instantly recognize Easton Ross and know her hot-as-sin husband is Jax Wilder. He's not an actor but everyone knows how Easton hired him back when she had a stalker. He not only protected her, but also caught her stalker and saved her life. And, of course, they fell madly in love and got married.

It was the kind of happily-ever-after that you found in books and movies.

"Chaz!" Easton exclaims. With her emerald, green eyes and shoulder-length raven curls, Easton's beauty is breath taking. And, in person, even more so. Now, instead of Cinderella, I begin to feel like one of the ugly stepsisters.

They swap air kisses and I glance at Jax who is tall, dark and broody looking. A bad boy who fell in love with a movie star and who can wear a suit better than James Bond. He slants a look at Chaz, not overly thrilled to be sharing his gorgeous wife and I notice the tattoo on the side of his neck, peeking out from his shirt collar. It looks like a dagger, but I can't be sure.

"You remember my husband, Jax Wilder," she says.

"Of course," Chaz says, and he and Jax shake hands. "Good to see you again, Jax. How's Platinum Security doing?"

"Busy, but good. Thanks for asking."

Chaz turns to me. "Jax runs a security firm and Easton was one of his clients a couple of years ago. And the rest is history." He turns back to them and introduces me. "This is Taylor, my girlfriend."

We exchange greetings and I can't help but admire how good they look together. And I feel my heart speed up when he calls me his girlfriend. Even though it isn't true, I like the sound of it.

"I love your dress," Easton tells me.

"Thank you," I say, excited to hear the compliment. After all, this is Easton Ross, America's Sweetheart. "And I love yours." It had a vintage look and fit her curves like a glove.

"Taylor is an amazing ballerina," Chaz says.

When I hear the pride in his voice, my heart swells a bit. No one has ever said anything so simple yet so sweet like that. No one has ever made me feel so special.

"Really?" Easton asks, green eyes widening. "That requires an inordinate amount of skill and training. How long have you been doing ballet?"

"Just over 17 years."

"Damn," Jax says. "That's impressive."

"Taylor is auditioning for companies right now. We're hoping she gets a position at the American Ballet Company. You'll have to come to a performance."

"We would love that," Easton says.

We chat for another minute and then it's time to go to our seats. I wave goodbye and feel a little starstruck when Easton gives me a hug. Then, she and Jax saunter away.

"I just love her," I admit. "I've seen all her movies."

"Yet, you've seen none of mine," he comments in a dry voice.

"You do action stuff. She mostly does romantic comedies."

"And what did you think about Jax?" he asks carefully.

If I'm not mistaken, I hear what almost sounds like jealousy. "He's very intense."

"He used to be a cop."

"Oh, I totally see that. He looks like he could kick someone's ass without even breaking a sweat." I glance over at Chaz and see him frown. "But he's not my type," I add. "I like the pretty-boy actors more."

A smile curves his mouth. Then, at the top of the huge theatre, in front of everyone, he pulls me close and kisses me again. Even though I know we're only acting, a part of me melts just a little. Like when you leave a stick of butter out on a hot day. The way his mouth moves over mine, the minty taste of him. Just when I think my legs are going to buckle, he ends the kiss and gives me a devastating grin.

I can feel people staring at us as we make our way over to our seats and sit down. "I think that just got everyone's attention," I murmur.

"Good," he says and snags my hand. Then, he lifts it up and places a kiss on its back. "You're doing really well tonight."

For a moment, I bask in the attention and then the lights go down. Chaz holds my hand through the entire movie, and I find that I'm enjoying our arrangement probably more than I should. I'm not used to a man showering me with attention and kisses. It's all so new and I'm really beginning to like it.

I sneak a glance over at his handsome profile and a wicked thought goes through my head. Maybe I shouldn't have been so adamant about the no-sex clause. I'm finding out so many things that I like about Chaz and maybe we can explore things a little further.

Before I know it, the movie ends, and everyone claps. For the last two hours, my mind has been on everything but the film and I'm not sure I could even tell you what it was about.

I've been too busy re-living Chaz's two kisses.

Chaz guides me back outside and, as we wait for our SUV to pull up, he's so attentive. Always making sure I'm taken care of and touching me, holding my hand, brushing a strand of hair back and over my shoulder.

It's the most perfect night I have ever had.

Then, we get in the car, and he instantly let's go of my hand and slides away, putting extra space between us. After being so close all night, it suddenly feels like the Grand Canyon separates us. Chaz is suddenly all business and, for a moment, my head spins at the complete 180 degree turn. Cool and distant, he pulls his cell phone out of a pocket and checks his texts or emails. He doesn't say a word to me as the car pulls into traffic.

I'm not going to lie. I'm a little taken aback by how easily he disengages from me. While here I am, lost in thoughts about those perfect kisses we shared.

Finally, after what seems like an eternity, he looks over at me. "You did good tonight. We definitely managed to get everyone's attention and in a positive way. Don't be surprised when you see yourself on the cover of the gossip magazines."

Wow, he really knows how to turn it off. *Like a damn light switch,* I think, my feelings hurt a little. I know they shouldn't be, and this is all a ruse, but I can't help it. I'm not an actress and it's harder for me to adjust and go from his kisses and attention to nothing at all.

Because right now, he's not even looking at me like a friend. More like an acquaintance whose name he can't quite remember.

It's all an agreement, I remind myself. *All fake and you need to keep your heart out of it.*

When we pull up to Sunset Terrace, I just blink, feeling a little lost. Even when we went out to dinner, he was charming and friendly. But now…

Now it's like he put up an icy wall between us.

"I'll call you tomorrow to go over the schedule for this week."

"Um, okay."

"Have a good night."

"You, too," I murmur and slip out of the car. As I watch it pull away, I feel confused. And I can't stop thinking about how real his kisses felt.

I have a sinking feeling that if I don't get it together and guard my heart, I'm going to be in a world of trouble.

Chapter Ten: Chaz

The moment Taylor gets out of the car, I drop my head back against the seat and close my eyes. *Shit.* This is going to be harder than I realized. I can't get those kisses out of my head and I'm starting to feel a very real attraction toward her.

Oh, who the hell am I kidding? My dick's hard and I wanted her from the moment I first saw her dancing at Club Noir. She's a breath of fresh air and makes me feel young and appreciated. When she looks up at me, I can see the interest and respect in her eyes.

Unlike my ex-wife, who used to spend most of her time glaring at me or talking down to me. Sabrina Destin was a six-month mistake that scarred me for life. Sure, she's beautiful and famous, but her heart, if in fact she does have one, is like a block of ice. I couldn't thaw it out and I seriously doubt any man would be able to.

The time we spent together was rocky and tumultuous. When we weren't fighting, we were ignoring each other because one or both of us was pissed off about something. And that led to a miserable, short-lived marriage. Maybe it would've dragged on longer if I hadn't found my wife in our bed with another man. I had wrapped filming early, flew home and caught them. I had a feeling she was going elsewhere since we'd stopped sleeping together, but I wasn't sure until I walked in on them. My gut still cramps up when I think about it and I've never been able to erase the disturbing image from my head.

Even though I knew our marriage wasn't going to last, it still hurt. I felt like a failure and was too concerned about what other people thought. Even though Sabrina drove me absolutely crazy, I did love her. At least in the beginning when we had a strong attraction and passionate relationship. But our inability to communicate and constant traveling left us with a rocky, unstable foundation. It didn't take long for it to crumble and for us to unravel.

I don't like to think about my time with Sabrina because it reminds me of how much she messed with my head and heart. I was only 28, completely naive and in love for the first time.

Now, I'm wiser and know that it takes more than great sex to have a strong relationship.

After we divorced, I vowed to avoid anything serious, never get married again and stick to my carefree bachelor lifestyle. I never want to be that vulnerable again.

I'm discovering that being with Taylor feels easy and, dare I say, right. It's throwing me off and making me rethink my stance on relationships. I have no intention of breaking our contract or making things awkward behind closed doors. God knows, she's been quite upfront about her no-sex rule and that's fine.

But a part of me can't help but wonder…

A virgin. I've never slept with a virgin before. Even when I was one. The women I normally invite back home or to my hotel room are far from innocent. They know exactly what they're getting into with me and have zero expectations once the sun comes up. Just that it's time to hit the road.

But I wouldn't mind getting to know Taylor on a more intimate level. If there was no contract and we just met and dated under normal circumstances, I'd be chomping at the bit to get her ass in my bed. I know I'd have to take it slow and court and seduce her, but the moment I had her naked, I would spend all night exploring her perfect ballerina body and introducing her to every last pleasure I could. Hell, she could sit on my face, pirouette in circles and I'd love every minute of it.

I shake my head and try to get my mind out of the gutter. Taylor is sweet and innocent, and she is the furthest thing from my usual type. I need to stick with my normal, experienced women who will come over for a quick, hard romp and then be on their merry way.

When the driver pulls up to my house, I tell him good night and slip out. *Time for a cold shower,* I think, and head inside.

The next day, I text Taylor and invite her over for dinner so we can go over my upcoming schedule. I need her to be available for a few different things, but as I'm looking through my calendar, I get an idea. Instead of attending a charity event and a couple of dinners, I should kick this into high gear.

I decide I'm going to introduce Taylor Quinn to the world and start our whirlwind romance off right. And what better place to do that than the City of Lights? She will have to take a couple of days off so hopefully she doesn't mind. But, hell, who would mind being swept away to Paris for a long weekend?

The more I think about it, the more excited I get. I call Brand and tell him my plan. He doesn't sound overly thrilled, but I need his help and give him a shopping list of things to pick up for me for tonight.

When Brand arrives, I help him carry all the bags into the kitchen and we start organizing things. He's looking at me with a funny expression and, as I'm unraveling a strand of lights, I pause.

"What?" I ask.

He shrugs. "You're going to have an awful lot of trouble. Guess I'm just wondering why?"

"It's not any trouble," I say and look at all the French-themed props and food I had him buy. "I just thought it would be kind of a fun surprise for her." My gaze wanders over to the Eiffel Tower replica that is almost three feet tall. *Oh, shit,* I think. *Maybe I went a little overboard.* "You don't think she'll like it? Is it too much? Am I jumping on the couch like Tom Cruise?"

"Actually, quite the opposite. I think she'll love it. It's all very...thoughtful. Are you feeling okay?"

I roll my eyes. "Lucky you're my brother or I would've fired your ass years ago."

"No, you would not have because I'm the only one who tells you the truth. I don't kiss your ass and tell you everything is fine when it isn't."

"True and I do appreciate it. Even though there are times when I wish you'd keep your opinions to yourself."

He slugs my arm and I punch him right back. Sibling relationships are the craziest, most frustrating and wonderful thing in the world. Especially my bond with Brandon. We've been best friends since he was born, we know what the other is thinking before he even speaks and we've almost killed each other a couple of times, but then immediately made up. It's been a wild ride and I wouldn't trade him for the world.

I know he's the only person that I can always count on, 100 percent of the time. Through all the ups and downs of my career and all the Hollywood bullshit, he's been there for me. And I'm there for him. Whatever my little brother needs, I will provide, no questions asked. We have each other's backs and, in a town like this, that's priceless.

We carry everything into the dining room, and I put the Eiffel Tower replica in the corner. Okay, maybe it's a little much, but I think it's fun. Actually, I think Taylor will think it's fun and that's why I'm doing all of this. I could've simply bought the plane tickets and been done with it. But, just seeing the smile on her face when she walks in here will make it all worthwhile.

Brand helps me string up some twinkling lights and then set the table. After we're done, we take a step back and examine our work. "What do you think?" I ask.

"It looks like Paris took a huge dump all over your dining room."

"Good. That's what it should look like." I nod my approval then tap my finger on the edge of the table. "Something's missing."

"More lights?" he teases.

I frown and think. He picked up literally everything that represents Paris, but I feel like there should be something else. "Oh, shit, I know!"

"What?"

I tell Brand exactly what we're missing, and he goes off to secure it.

Excellent. Now there is no way in the world that Taylor would not want to go on this trip with me. I've covered all my bases and made it far too hard for her to say no. She's going to be the first one on that plane and I can't wait to see the look on her face tonight.

By the time evening rolls around, I'm nervous. I have no idea why and I feel like I'm about to jump out of my skin. When she texts me that she's here, I jog over to the front door and reach for the knob. Brand left to go meet the guys for dinner and a few drinks, so it'll be just the two of us and I'm really looking forward to her reaction to all of this.

"Hi," I say, absurdly happy to see her.

"Hi," she answers back.

Her voice sounds cooler than usual. "Everything okay?" I ask.

"Sure. Just here for our business dinner and to obtain the upcoming schedule," she says and breezes inside.

I pause, not sure I care for her tone, and I know I shouldn't get annoyed because it is a business relationship, but I can't help it. Hopefully, she'll loosen up after my big announcement. "It's in the dining room," I say and walk her across the foyer.

When we reach the dim room with strands of twinkling lights hanging from the ceiling, her eyes widen in surprise. She looks at the spread on the table-- wine, cheese, bread, fruit-- and then at the screen on the wall where images of Paris flash. There's some low French music playing in the background and she walks over to the Eiffel Tower in the corner and touches it.

"What is all this?" she asks and turns around to face me.

Did I go overboard? I wonder. Suddenly, I feel a little foolish and wonder if I should've just handed her a plane ticket. *Too late now.* I clear my throat and pull her chair out. "Have a seat, mademoiselle."

Taylor sits down and watches me with a curious look as I sit next to her.

"So, I, ah, was thinking earlier and decided we should kick off our romance in the most romantic city in the world." When she raises a brow, I clarify, "In Paris."

For a moment, she doesn't say anything. "You want me to go to Paris, France, with you?"

"Tomorrow. Our flight leaves in the morning."

I notice her chew on her lower lip and hesitate.

"What's wrong? You don't want to go to Paris?"

"No, I'd love to go to Paris. This is all just really sudden, and I have classes. How long are we going for?"

"I already called your teacher. You're excused from your classes for a few days."

"What?" Taylor lets out a breath that sounds part annoyed and part frustrated. "You should've let me make that decision and talk to my teacher myself. How did you even know who-" She runs a hand through her fiery hair. "Never mind, it doesn't matter. The point is, just because I'm pretending to be your girlfriend doesn't mean you start making decisions for me. And, it clearly states in the contract that I will not have to sacrifice my ballet classes."

"It's just a few days."

"That's not the point."

"So, what are you saying? You're not going?" I feel myself starting to get pissed off. I went to a lot of trouble, and she doesn't seem to be appreciating it at all.

"No. I'm saying, next time ask me before you start booking flights."

"Fine," I relent. I slouch down in my chair and sulk. I really thought this would all be fun for her, and it's turned into a mess. I don't know why I even bothered, and I feel like an idiot.

"What's this?" she asks and pulls out the envelope tucked beneath her plate.

I give her a half-shrug.

She opens the envelope and pulls out two tickets to the Paris Ballet. "Oh, my God." Her blue gaze snaps up and meets mine. "Are you serious?"

"I thought you might like to go, but we don't have to-"

"Of course, I want to go! This is unbelievable!" Her gaze moves over all the cheesy decorations and then she gives me a little smile. "I'm sorry I wasn't more excited at first. You really put a lot of effort into this."

"Not really," I lie, and she arches a brow. "I mean, a little." I reach for the bottle of red wine and fill my glass. "Want some?" When she nods, I pour her some, too.

She takes a sip and watches the different, iconic images of Paris flicker across the screen for a minute. "Why did you do all this?"

"I thought it would be fun for you. Apparently, I was wrong."

"You weren't wrong, Chaz. But if I have to play by your rules then I expect you to give me the same consideration."

I realize she has a point and I sit up taller. "You're right. I should've talked to you first. I guess I just kind of wanted it to be a surprise."

Taylor gives me a funny look. "But, why? It's just me and you right now. No cameras or reporters or paparazzi. No show to put on for anyone."

Shit, she has a point. Why did I go to all this trouble? *Fuck.* I may as well be on national TV right now jumping up and down on the goddamn couch. Suddenly, I feel like a fool, and I'm pissed at Brand for letting me do this. He should've told me not to do it. "I guess because I'm an idiot," I finally say and pluck a slice of cheese off a tray.

When she reaches for a strawberry, she looks thoughtful. "You're not an idiot," she says.

"Thanks," I mumble and take another sip of wine.

She chuckles. "I just didn't see this coming."

"See what's coming?"

"That you have a sentimental side."

"No, I don't," I immediately deny. I am not the kind of man who secretly watches Hallmark movies or chick flicks or picks up my girlfriend's romance novel and sneaks a peek. I watch ESPN, action movies and I read thrillers with badass heroes who shoot guns and beat the crap out of bad guys.

"I think you do," she insists.

"Shows how well you know me," I scoff, refusing to admit that I am anything but an alpha, macho man who does what he wants, when he wants.

But she just gives me this little knowing smirk. "Okay, so maybe I don't know you that well yet. Other than the fact that you're a bit bossy and controlling."

I narrow my eyes. "Give me those tickets," I growl and grab for them. "I'm returning them."

"No!" she screeches and leaps up, clutching them to her chest.

I circle the table, heading for her, and she gives another squeal and races around, staying out of my reach. When I fake a move to the left and then run to the right, she spins and takes off in the opposite direction. And, as I'm chasing her around the large table, my brother walks into the room with John, Ozzy and Lang.

The moment they see Taylor, I notice all the sly looks and smirks.

"Hey," I say to my entourage and then glance over at Taylor who gives them a little wave. "Guys, this is Taylor. Taylor, you met Brand, and this is John, Ozzy and Langston."

"Nice to meet you," she says, and they all greet her.

"We're going to watch the game," Brand says. "Sorry for the interruption, but they wanted to be momentarily transported to Paris, too."

I hear some snickers and glare at them.

"It's beautiful," Ozzy says and pretends to shed a tear. Then, he leans in a little closer and, under his breath says, "Well? Are you going to accept the grandpa role or…"?

He lets his voice trail off suggestively and waggles his eyebrows, sending a look over in Taylor's direction.

"I'm securing the deal right now," I say. "And, trust me, there won't be any grandfatherly roles in my near future."

"That's my man," Ozzy says and slaps me on the back.

Chapter Eleven: Taylor

After my magical, pretend evening in Paris, I go home and start packing for the real thing. I can't believe that tomorrow at this time, I will be in Europe in the most romantic city in the world.

With my fake boyfriend.

I've never been to Paris so it would have been nice to do this trip with a real boyfriend, but I suppose this is the next best thing. And Chaz was friendly all night, not cool like he'd turned after the movie premiere. When I gave him a hard time about missing my ballet classes, his feelings almost seemed hurt. I can't believe how much effort he took, and it was pretty sweet.

That's the problem, though. I have no idea what is going on in his head and I don't like his hot/cold attitude. Half the time, he treats me like a real girlfriend and the other half like I'm a stranger. It's a little hard to predict how he will act each time I see him and that's a little exhausting.

The next morning, a car takes us to LAX and I am so excited. "I can't believe I'm going to Paris," I say as we step onto the airplane. "This is freaking unbelievable!"

"Have you ever been?"

"No. This is crazy."

Our seats are right upfront in first class, and I stretch out in the large, comfy seat. A moment later, a flight attendant hands me a glass of champagne. *Wow.* Talk about chic.

Chaz looks over at me and clinks his glass against mine. "To the City of Lights and the beginning of our romance."

I take a sip and buckle up. He seems to be in a really good mood and so am I which makes the flight literally fly. We talk almost the entire way and I find out that I'm really enjoying getting to know him. We talk about our families, favorite things, worst experiences and literally everything else under the sun.

When we finally take a break from chatting, I sit back in my seat and look out the window. It's been a long, enjoyable flight, but I'm ready to get my feet back on solid ground. The pilot announces that we'll be landing soon, and I watch as the ground gets closer and closer.

After we land and collect our luggage, a car waits to take us to the most amazing place I have ever seen. The Four Seasons Hotel George V is an art-deco landmark built in 1928 and right in the heart of the city.

I stop and look up at the huge building. It takes my breath away. The driver from the hotel smiles when he sees my awe.

"She is a beauty, no?" he asks.

"Stunning. I can't believe we're staying here."

"You will have a wonderful time," he promises.

Our personal attendant, Yves, meets us and takes us up to the penthouse suite. I can't believe I gave Chaz a hard time about coming here. This is the most magnificent place I have even seen and when the door to the room opens, I almost fall over.

Yves takes us from room to room on a tour of the oversized suite. He points out Baccarat Crystal glassware, a plasma-screen television hidden behind a black mirror, a bookcase full of antique books and a private bar. Then, he ushers us onto the outdoor terrace with sweeping views of the city. The first thing I see is the Eiffel Tower and my jaw drops. "I can't believe this," I whisper.

I glance over at Chaz, and he smiles. I guess he's used to staying at places like this, but I am most certainly not. When Yves begins to point out several other iconic buildings, I lean forward and rest my arms on the black wrought-iron balcony.

"Over there, you can see the Sacré-Coeur Basilica and there are the roofs of the Opéra, the Madeleine, the Panthéon and Les Invalides."

It's absolutely breath taking.

After assuring us he is available for anything we need, Yves leaves and I wander through the suite, taking in the sumptuous living room, private conservatory, full marble bath and, finally, the King-size four-poster bed. *Only one bed*, I realize, but for some odd reason, I don't really care at this moment.

"Well, Twinkle Toes, how do you like our room?"

"Room? This is bigger than my apartment!" I exclaim and he chuckles.

"So, you're glad you came?"

"Yes. It's all really too much. But I love it," I add with a huge smile.

"I'm glad. Your first time in Paris should be special. Something you'll always remember."

His words seem to hold a deeper meaning and I feel my heart kick against my ribs. *My first time…*

Paris would be an amazing place to lose my virginity. How many girls back home can say they lost it in the City of Lights? Not many. "So, uh, what's the plan?" I ask.

"Well, since you've never been here, I figured we could be tourists. Yves has a car waiting whenever you're ready and he's going to show us the sights."

I nod enthusiastically. "I'd love that."

"Great. Why don't we freshen up and I'll let him know we'll meet him downstairs in 20 minutes?"

"Okay," I say. Then, I grab my cosmetics case and head into the bathroom which is bigger than my living room and is full of fresh flowers and there's even a statue up on a pedestal in the corner. I spend a few minutes checking everything out and then touch up my makeup. I also decide to change my outfit. I'm in Paris now and I want to dress up more. I slip on a dress with a little sweater and cute ballet flats.

After I'm ready, I find Chaz in the living room talking on the phone to his brother. When he sees me, he concludes their conversation and tells him he'll call him later. Chaz stands up and looks really handsome with a smart casual look. He wears a fitted, lightweight sweater under a tailored blazer and a nice pair of jeans. When he stands up and slides his sunglasses on, I feel heat slither down low between my thighs. *Um, yum. He looks absolutely edible.* Just like the movie star that he is.

"Ready?"

I nod and we meet Yves out in front of the hotel. For the next couple of hours, he drives us by all the things I've always heard about when people speak of Paris-- the Champs Elysée's, the Eiffel Tower, the Arc de Triomphe, Moulin Rouge, Notre Dame, The Louvre, cathedrals, cafes and flower marts. It's all utterly breath taking and whenever I squeal about something, Yves pulls over and lets us get out and explore.

"I'm sorry we don't have more time," Chaz says. "I feel like you're getting the abbreviated tour."

"No, it's wonderful. All of it," I say and twirl beneath the arches of the Eiffel Tower. "Let's take a picture!"

Chaz hands Yves his phone and we stand in a perfect spot. Several people recognize him-- I always know by the furious whispering and feminine shrieks-- and they begin to descend on us. But, first, Chaz pulls me into his arms, we press our cheeks together and smile. As Yves snaps a few photos, I feel the rough scruff on Chaz's face and his muscular arms wrapped around me.

And it feels so right.

Chaz turns and his bright cobalt eyes meet mine. Then, he takes my face in his large hands and kisses me thoroughly. And I lose track of the fans and the cameras clicking. All I can feel is Chaz's warm mouth moving over mine, slow and sultry.

And I want more.

When I open my mouth and touch his lips with my tongue, he hisses in a breath and pulls back. "We have an audience," he reminds me.

"Sorry," I whisper, hands clenching the lapels of his suit jacket.

"Don't ever apologize for kissing me." He rubs the tip of his nose against mine. "I love it."

I swallow hard and then he releases me and greets the people waiting to meet him and take more pictures. I can't get over how handsome he looks and my stomach flutters. God, I love kissing him. I'm looking forward to locking lips with him quite a few more times before this trip is over. I also can't help but think about that big king-size bed up in the suite.

Do I dare? I wonder. If I try to seduce him, I honestly don't know how he will react. Will he spurn my advances when we're alone and remind me that this is merely a business arrangement? Or, will he pull me into his arms and kiss me senseless.

God, I hope the latter. I can't imagine offering him my virginity and then he rejects me. I would be humiliated. The problem is, I can't ever tell if he's being sincere or just acting.

After spending some time with his fans, he heads back over to me and slips his hand into mine. "Ready to get some dinner?"

I nod and realize that I'm starving. But, with all of the excitement, I hadn't thought about food all day.

"There are a few really great restaurants back at the hotel."

"Okay, sounds good," I tell him. We get back in the car and Yves tells us to change while he arranges our table at Le Cinq. I only have two nice dresses and brought both of them because I had no idea what we'd be doing. I'm so glad I did, I think, as I open the closet and reach for the black cocktail dress. It's elegant, yet classic, with a sweetheart neckline and fits like a glove. The top is sheer, and the illusion neckline makes it a little sexy while still being covered up. I slip into a pair of black heels and hope that I look alright.

When I walk back into the living room, Chaz is waiting. He looks amazing in a black tailored suit and tie, and I get the urge to rumple it up a bit. He freezes when he sees me and his gaze dips appreciatively. I feel my cheeks heat up as he walks over and takes both of my hands in his. "You look so beautiful."

"Thank you. And you look quite dashing."

"Dashing?" He quirks a brow.

"I thought that sounded a little more refined than what I was thinking."

He pulls me a step closer. "And what may I ask, were you thinking?"

"That you look hot."

He laughs and places a kiss on the back of both my hands. "C'mon, Bun-Head."

I burst out laughing. "I'm not even wearing a bun."

When he reaches out and lifts a lock of my hair, I suddenly go quiet. "So fiery," he murmurs. "I've never seen hair this color. It's red, orange and gold all melted together."

I notice his breathing quickens and I wait to see what he'll do next. But then he drops the strand and collects himself. "We should go downstairs."

We head back down and walk over to two wrought-iron doors that lead into Le Cinq Restaurant. Like the rest of the hotel, it's stunning. Spacious and full of fresh flowers, the room is decorated in shades of gold and gray and it feels like we're about to dine in a private chateau. There are gold-gilded chairs and large Regency style mirrors with gold leafing. It's elegant and rich and lovely. *What am I doing here?*

"I can't believe I'm about to eat dinner here," I whisper as we sit down.

"Why?"

I place the cloth napkin on my lap and look around, eyes wide. "I'm used to frozen mac and cheese. I'm guessing they don't serve that here."

"No, Sugar Plum. They do not."

"This is the kind of place where they drizzle sauces all over your plate and make it really pretty to make up for the tiny portions, huh?"

Chaz barks out a laugh. Then, he leans closer and whispers, "To make up for the really big prices, too."

I look over the menu and my choices look like seafood, lamb or beef. I'm not really feeling any of those, so I order the regional cheese plate and seasonal green salad.

"Salad?" Chaz says. He eyes me for a minute. "Do you want to eat somewhere else?"

"Oh, no. This is beautiful."

"Are you sure?"

I nod. "It's sweet of you to offer, though."

When the waiter brings us a bottle of red wine, Chaz tells me that the wine cellar below us has more than 50,000 bottles.

"That's insane," I say. Whatever he ordered is absolutely delicious and I enjoy every sip. Dinner is beyond lovely and for dessert we share some kind of crispy vanilla wafer crepes and, oh, my goodness, they melt in my mouth.

After we eat, we return to our room where a bottle of champagne chills in a bucket on the terrace. Chaz glances down at his watch then nods over at the Eiffel Tower. "Watch," he says. "The light show is going to start."

As he pops the champagne, I walk over to the railing and gaze out over the city. Chaz moves up beside me, hands me a glass and we sip it. Suddenly, the entire tower begins to twinkle with white lights.

I gasp. "It's like it's sparkling!" The light show is so magical that I can't quite catch my breath. "Oh, Chaz, it's unbelievable."

I watch the light show until it ends and then realize that Chaz is watching me instead of the tower. When I turn toward him, I can't help but smile. "Thank you," I say. "Being here...with you...it's been surreal. I feel like I'm dreaming."

"You aren't dreaming, Taylor," he says and cups my face.

My heart starts to beat wildly, and I want him to kiss me so badly that I can't stand it anymore. I set my glass down and, after he does the same, I launch myself into his arms. Our mouths crash, lips moving, opening, and our tongues glide against one another, exploring. I wrap my arms around his neck and pull him closer, losing myself in the taste and feel of him.

It's all too good and Paris makes me forget all about our contract. Right now, I'm with a man who is getting harder and harder to resist. *So, why should I resist?* Today has been the best day I have ever had and now I want to remember tonight the same way-- as the best night of my life.

I feel his hands move up and down and then toy with my zipper. But he doesn't lower it. "Do it," I whisper, but I can feel his hesitation.

"Taylor…"

When I begin to softly kiss his neck, I know his resistance is crumbling when he groans. Then, he sinks his fingers into my hair and tilts my head back, forcing me to look up into his hot blue gaze. I can see the question there and I nod. "Yes, please, Chaz."

"Please what?" he asks in a low, unsteady voice. "Say it."

"Please, take me to bed."

With a growl, Chaz sweeps me up and carries me back into the room. He sets me down next to the bed, turns me around and reaches for the zipper. He pulls it down oh-so-slowly and my heart thunders so hard I feel like it might explode. Then, he tugs the dress down, slides it over my hips and it falls to the floor.

He moves up behind me, moves my hair to the side and begins to kiss my neck. I melt back against his chest and sigh.

"You smell so good," he says between kisses. "Like peaches and cream."

Then, he straightens up and turns me around. His gaze soaks up every detail of my strapless black satin bra and panties and I can't help but feel self-conscious. "You're so elegant and graceful looking. Yet, there is so much power in this body."

When he runs his hands up my arms, I shiver.

"Are you sure, Taylor?"

Instead of answering, I reach for his jacket and push it off his broad shoulders. "I don't ever want to forget tonight," I say. "Help me remember it forever."

Chaz yanks his tie off and then starts on his buttons. When he shrugs out of the shirt, my eyes lower to his perfect chest. Holy hell, I didn't expect him to be so ripped. I reach out and caress the muscles and grooves on his abdomen. I feel him tense and then relax as I explore every ridge.

The moment my hands skim the edge of his trousers, he reaches down and unbuckles his belt. Then, he drops his pants, and I can't help but get an eyeful. *Oh, my.* He's ready, but I'm not quite there yet. He must know this because he lowers me back on the bed, moves up over me and kisses me. It's slow and sultry and sends tingles down to my toes.

"I'm going to explore every inch of you," he promises and reaches around to unsnap my bra. I suck in a breath when it falls aside and feel my cheeks flame. "So damn beautiful. Do you have any idea how perfect you are?"

But I shake my head. "No…"

"Yes," he insists, hands cupping my breasts. "So absolutely perfect."

When he lowers his head and pulls a nipple into his mouth, I arch up and sigh. He moves from one to the other, worshipping, sucking, driving me crazy. I dig my fingers into the hard muscles of his shoulders and squirm. Heat floods my body and I want more.

His mouth drags down the valley between my breasts, tongue swirling around my navel, and I glance down, frozen with heat. *How is that even possible?* I wonder. He looks up at me, grazes his teeth along the waistband of my panties and then bites down on the elastic edge and pulls. I swallow hard as they slide down my legs and disappear.

Chaz sits back on his heels and stares down at my naked body. "So lovely," he rasps and reaches for a leg. He lifts it, slides it over his shoulder and begins to kiss his way up my inside thigh.

Oh. My.

I don't know what to do so I just grab a handful of the comforter and ball it up in my fist. When his hot mouth closes over my centre, I gasp and try to squeeze my legs together, but he doesn't let me. Instead, he pushes my thighs apart further to give him better access and I just blink as wave after wave of sensation begins to make my lower body throb.

That very talented mouth of his seems to know just what to do and I am at his mercy as he licks, strokes and swirls his tongue through my folds and around my most sensitive parts. When he sucks my clit into his mouth, I jerk up and slam a fist against the bed. "Chaz," I gasp.

"Let go, baby," he murmurs.

"I can't," I say, not sure how or what he means. All I know is the pressure is building, increasing steadily, and I'm left panting hard and writhing.

When he slides a finger inside me, I buck against his hand and try to deal with the pulsing need that washes over me. "I don't know…"

"You're so wet," he murmurs, fingers toying with me.

I glance down and he looks up, blue eyes blazing, and applies just the right amount of pressure. I cry out, throw my head back and feel all the tension explode and then dissolve into pleasure. It catches me off-guard and when the ripples stop, I can't move. I feel caught in a hazy cloud of utter contentment.

Chaz moves off the bed, retrieves a condom from his suitcase and then loses his boxer briefs. My gaze drops and I bite the inside of my cheek. He's very well-endowed and my nerves kick up a notch. I watch as he sheathes himself and then moves between my legs.

He must feel me tense up because he begins to kiss me, slow and unhurried, and I melt all over again. When he slides a hand down and strokes me, I can't believe how worked up I'm getting again. "You like this?" he asks.

"Mmm-hmm," I murmur and shift in restless anticipation.

"How about this?" He slides two fingers inside me and moves them in and out. My only answer is a somewhat strangled cry, and he chuckles. "I'll take that as a yes."

"You're, um, really good at this," I tell him.

I can feel him smile against my neck where he's sucking the sensitive skin there. "Oh, you just wait."

When I slide a foot along the back of his leg, he grabs my hips and positions me beneath him. "Just relax, okay?" he says, his long, thick length nudging at my entrance.

"I'll try."

"Don't try, just let go," he whispers and captures my mouth in a heated kiss as he pushes into my tight body.

Oh, my freaking God, I think, and arch up, opening to him.

Chapter Twelve: Chaz

As I sink into Taylor's tight, hot body, nothing has ever felt so good. Her body expands around me, trying to accommodate me, and I slide back out, giving her time to adjust. Then, I waste no time, and sink back into her wet warmth.

God, it's like I'm coming home or something. The strange thought flits across my mind as I push deeper and she clamps her legs around me, drawing me in and making these sexy whimpering noises that are starting to drive me crazy. I've been working hard to maintain my control, but I feel it begin to slip as I start to move, forcing myself to keep the pace slow and easy, but God Almighty, all I want to do is slam into her, possess her completely.

I know we're breaking our rule, ignoring the contract, and I'm not going to lie. I'm so fucking glad. I never thought taking her virginity would feel like this. Something protective inside of me takes over and I want to make this experience as good as I possibly can for her. *So far, so good,* I think, gauging her reactions and responses.

I remember back to when we were going over the contract and what I said.

Think of me more like a Daddy figure. I'll make sure you're taken care of while we're together. I'm very generous, Taylor.

I grit my teeth and force myself to keep the steady rhythm up for a bit longer. Then, I lift her hips, changing the angle, and thrust harder, faster. I make sure I'm hitting her body just right and when she clenches around me and cries out, I watch the orgasm slam through her. Now that I know she's taken care of, just like I promised, I lose myself in my own release.

And it's powerful. "*Christ,*" I hiss, shuddering and exploding. The intensity catches me off-guard, but nothing has ever felt so damn good. I collapse beside her and bury my face in her long, red hair.

When I get my breathing under control, I slip out of bed, take care of the condom and then return to her side. She still looks a little dazed and I tuck a strand of fiery hair behind her ear. "You okay?"

She turns her head and gazes at me with a wondrous look in her blue eyes. "That was amazing."

The edge of my mouth curves and I pull her into my arms, gathering her into my embrace and savoring the curve of her body against mine. "There's more where that came from," I promise and kiss her temple. We both fall asleep almost instantly and my dreams are filled with dancing Sugar Plum Fairies.

The next morning, I order room service and we enjoy coffee, juice, fresh fruit and pastries outside on the terrace with the Eiffel Tower soaring up in the background. I never considered myself overly romantic, but Paris has a way of making you believe in magic again.

I watch Taylor sip her orange juice and munch on a flaky croissant drizzled in chocolate. Her legs are curled up beneath her and she's in the big fluffy, white robe provided by the hotel, looking out at the city.

"It's so beautiful," she says. Then, she turns her attention to me and smiles. And damn if my heart doesn't jolt within my chest. "I love Paris."

I take a drink of coffee and consider her words. I'm glad I was able to make this trip memorable for her. In more ways than one. I don't know about her, but I can't stop thinking about last night and the way her body felt wrapped around me. *Too right.*

"What do you want to do today?" she asks.

"Well, we have the ballet tonight," I say, and she nods eagerly. "I thought we could do some shopping. Get you something new to wear?"

"Really? I'd love that!"

Her enthusiasm is contagious, and I decide that I'm going to spoil her rotten today. I'm going to buy her anything she even glances at and ship it all back to Sunset Terrace wrapped up in a big red bow. I doubt anyone has ever spoiled her like I'm going to and that makes me happy.

"We should get ready, and I'll have Yves meet us downstairs in an hour."

"I need to take a shower," she says and pops up.

When she walks by me, I grab her hand, turn it over and place an open-mouthed kiss in her palm. "Maybe later, we can take one together."

Her blue eyes widen then turn sultry. "Maybe."

My mouth edges up and I spank her ass. "Go. Before I ravage you right here on this table."

With a squeal, she scurries away, and I have a feeling today is going to be a really good day.

I have Yves drive us over to the crème de la crème of couture where we have an appointment at Chanel. He turns onto Avenue Montaigne, part of the "Golden Triangle," and suddenly the air feels more rarefied as we enter the territory of the world's most famous fashion houses: Hermès, Saint Laurent, Ferragamo, Givenchy, Prada, Gucci, Bulgari, Dior, Chanel and many more. They have flagship stores, haute couture showrooms and by-invitation-only salons here along the enclave of shaded streets and pale marble mansions.

When Yves pulls up to 31 Rue Cambon, Taylor's jaw drops. "Are you joking?"

She's practically drooling on the window, and I chuckle. "I take it you appreciate Chanel?"

"Oh, my God, it's iconic. I've never owned anything by Chanel."

Good, I think. "Well, let's change that."

A young woman meets us at the door and ushers us inside. "Welcome to Chanel, Monsieur Stone," she says. "I'm Amélie."

"A pleasure. And, this is Mademoiselle Quinn," I say, and the women exchange a greeting.

"We have your room waiting and an array of potential outfits for you to try on for the ballet tonight, Mademoiselle Quinn."

As we walk through the salon, I don't notice anything about the renowned fashion house. I'm too busy watching Taylor's face and ever-changing expressions. She gazes up at the curved ceiling, columns with tall mirrors, antique consoles and the modernist staircase.

Amélie points to the staircase as we walk past. "CoCo would get nervous before fashion shows, so she used to hide on the stairs, out of sight, and smoke her cigarette."

The scent of lilies fills the air and vases filled to the brim sit on every table.

"The boutique is here on the ground floor; the design studio is located on the third floor and the haute couture ateliers are on the upper floors where seamstresses make made-to-measure outfits for a handful of clients."

Amélie guides us to a spacious private fitting room where eight dresses hang up in lit-up glass cabinets with gilded frames. I sit down in a white, overstuffed armchair beside a table with gilded bronze legs in the shape of wheatsheaves. I lean back, lace my fingers and prepare to watch my girl get spoiled.

When Amélie tells Taylor to get undressed she gives me a nervous look and I smirk. *Seriously?* After last night, she's going to play shy. I just raise a brow and my smile widens. "Let me know if you need any help, Sugar Plum," I say.

Taylor's cheeks heat up and she clears her throat. "I think I'm okay."

But the game turns on me quickly when she makes a production out of unbuttoning her shirt and shimmying out of her skirt. She gives me a wicked little smile as she stands there in her heels, a black satin bra and matching panties. My cock surges against my zipper and I stifle a groan. If this is a sign of things to come, I have a feeling that this is going to be a long and torturous fitting for me to sit through.

The first dress Amélie slips over her head is a black dress that flares out with crinoline underneath. Taylor steps in front of the 3-way mirror and admires it from every angle. "It's so pretty," she says and does a little spin.

I might think "spin" in my head, but when Taylor spins, it's more intricate. It's precise, graceful and full of technique.

"You are a ballerina, no?" Amélie asks.

Taylor nods.

"I can tell. Your physique is lithe and strong. So much power and beauty. And, you have an air of grace about you."

"Thank you," Taylor says demurely.

"Let's try the next one."

After she tries on all the dresses, I know which one my favorite is, but I defer to her and Amélie to decide. Taylor walks back over to the cabinet and goes straight to the one I would've chosen. "This one," she whispers almost reverently.

It's a silvery-white gown with matching, dainty rosebuds over the tee-length skirt which poofs out. The design is feminine and reminds me of something that an innocent ballerina would wear. *And that's my Taylor.*

"A lovely choice. And, Monsieur Stone," she asks and turns to me. "Which is your favorite?"

"That one," I say, and Taylor smiles.

"Is it, really?" she asks.

I nod, liking that we're on the same page. Because right now, I have some very specific ideas going through my mind about how I'd like to spend our last night in Paris. After the ballet and when I have her back up in the suite, all to myself.

I know I'm playing a dangerous game, but it's Paris for fuck's sake. I think we should just enjoy ourselves and not be thinking about a contract. In fact, we should probably step things up.

"Let's put it back on and choose some shoes, shall we?"

Taylor looks over at me and I nod. When I do something, it's not half-ass. I'd never expect her to wear some cheap shoes with that expensive dress. I like how she looks to me for permission, though. It puts a few more interesting thoughts in my head.

Later, I tell myself. Now, I just enjoy watching her spin around in her new dress and try on shoes. They end up choosing a delicate matching heel with pearls around the ankle. Amélie suggests a pearl necklace to "show off her graceful, swan-like throat" and I nod. At this point, I'll buy anything. I just want to get out of here and move on to the next store.

I just hope Taylor doesn't freak out.

After they wrap everything up and I pay a small fortune, we get back in the waiting car and I tell Yves to take us over to the Cartier flagship store on Rue de la Paix.

Taylor's head snaps over and she turns to face me. "Cartier?"

"I think we should step things up. Don't you?"

She looks like she's at a loss for words, trying to wrap her head around everything that's happening. But then she gives me the most dazzling smile I have ever seen. "Are you proposing?" she murmurs in a low, teasing voice.

I reach out and slide across the seat and onto my lap. "You know what? I think I am." I nibble on her ear lobe, and she squirms. "Careful," I say in a low voice. "After watching you prance around half-naked for the past two hours, I'm feeling highly aroused."

"Really?" she whispers. Her blue eyes glow with a naughty light as she drops her hand over the front of my trousers. She makes a humming noise in the back of her throat and lightly massages me and it's nearly my undoing.

I grit my teeth and catch her hand, pulling it back up. "Later," I manage to say, trying to ignore the throbbing going on below my belt. She cups my face and pulls me in for a long, heated kiss.

I push my tongue between her lips and circle it inside her mouth while my hands dip under her skirt and slide over her satin-covered ass. I'd like to explore more, but with Yves so close, it's not a good idea.

Besides, we're pulling up to Cartier and it wouldn't be a good look to get caught with my hands in her underpants.

We get out and I lace my fingers through hers and we walk through the front door. I guide her over to a case full of diamond engagement rings and enjoy the way her face lights up. "Pick one."

"Seriously?"

I nod and a sales associate walk over and asks if we'd like to see anything. I think I see a glimmer of recognition pass through her eyes, but she's a complete professional. "We just got engaged," I say.

"Mes sincères félicitations."

"Thank you," Taylor says.

"What catches your eye?" I ask.

"They're all stunning," she says and leans closer. We wait while she checks every ring out. Then, she points to one in particular. "But something about this one…"

"A brilliant choice," the associate says and removes it from the case. She lays it on a velvet cloth and Taylor looks over at me.

"Try it on," I encourage her.

Taylor very carefully picks it up and slides it onto her slim finger. Ironically, it's a perfect fit.

It's funny because it's the exact one I would've chosen. It's a round diamond, circled by other diamonds in a platinum setting.

"It's the Destinée solitaire," the associate says. Then, she explains the carat, color and clarity.

I lift Taylor's hand and turn it this way and that, letting the light fall on it so it sparkles with a brilliant fire. "It's like last night," Taylor says. "When the Eiffel Tower sparkled."

My gaze locks onto Taylor's and, for just a moment, it feels like my heart stops beating. "We'll take it," I say, unable to look away from her blue eyes.

"Chaz-"

"Don't say another word. It's yours." Then, I pull her into my arms and kiss her. Several people clap and offer their congratulations. Taylor blushes furiously, as usual, and I smirk. "I love when you blush," I murmur.

While I pay for the ring, she wanders around, admiring the jewelry in each case. They clean the ring up and make it more perfect than it already was and when they bring it back, all wrapped up and in a signature box and bag, I take it.

"Ready?" She nods and we thank them for their help. Once we're outside, a barrage of camera flashes goes off. It's weird because I kind of forgot that the whole point of coming here was to announce our love affair to the world. Now is the perfect moment to do that and I feel annoyed. Like I don't want to share this moment with anyone else but her.

But I know this is a prime photo op and I yank her into my arms and kiss her thoroughly. That photo-- me kissing Taylor, up on her tiptoes and leaning into me, the Cartier bag dangling near her hip-- makes it into every major magazine in the world.

And, just like that, the world knows that we are engaged. *Mission accomplished.*

Chapter Thirteen: Taylor

Tonight, is like a dream come true. I'm dressed in head-to-toe Chanel with a Cartier engagement ring on my finger on my way to the Paris Ballet with the most gorgeous, amazing, wonderful man I have ever met.

I feel like I'm dreaming, but I'm going to enjoy it thoroughly because I'm scared that I might wake up and it could end at any moment.

When the car pulls up to the curb out front of the Palais Garnier, my heart stops. Never in a million years did I think I would be here, and it means the world to me. Chaz opens the door for me, offers his hand and I step out and look up at the most amazing building.

The opera house seats almost 2,000 people and the extraordinary opulence of it is breath taking. A wave of emotion washes over me and I need a second to compose myself. Chaz glances over and gives me a concerned look. "What's wrong?" he asks.

A sheen of tears covers my eyes and I clasp my other hand over his. "Do you realize this is where *The Phantom of the Opera* happens?"

Chaz squeezes my hands. "And you called me sentimental."

I let out a shaky breath, place a hand against my chest and draw in a deep breath. "I can't believe I'm about to see the Paris Ballet perform." I look up at Chaz and smile. "Thank you."

"You're welcome."

Together, we walk into the magnificent building and into a sea of people. I'm so excited that I'm practically floating on air. We walk around the lobby and explore a bit before going to our seats. They're absolutely wonderful and I have a perfect view of the stage. I'm so excited that I can barely sit still.

"The Paris Opera Ballet is the oldest national ballet company," I say. "It's dance school is one of the most prestigious in the world and filters into the company. But, only if you're the best of the best. The school is fiercely competitive, and I read that more than 90 percent of candidates fail the entrance exam on their first attempt."

"I don't know how you do it," Chaz says. Then, he leans into my ear. "I still want to see you dance."

His warm breath at my ear makes my stomach somersault. "You've seen me dance."

"Not ballet."

"Maybe I'll have to do a private show for you later."

"How long is this performance?" he grumbles and glances down at his watch.

I push his arm and laugh. "Not long enough."

When the lights finally go down, I sit forward, and I'm absolutely mesmerized for the next two hours. The dancing is superb, flawless in every way. God, I hope I can be this good one day. I can't take my eyes off the performers and by the end, tears stream down my face. It's the most beautiful thing I've ever seen.

When Chaz notices, he squeezes my hand and pulls me up and into his arms. I wrap my arms around him and whisper, "Thank you, Chaz. I can't tell you how much this night means to me."

He pulls back and swipes a tear away. "Please, don't cry. I didn't want this to make you sad."

"I'm not sad. I'm crying because I'm so happy."

"Tears of joy?"

I nod. "Today has been perfect in every way."

"I think it's going to get even better," he promises.

We return to our suite at the hotel and when I walk out onto the terrace, I spot a bottle of champagne in a bucket of ice along with two delicious-looking desserts. "I could really get used to this," I say. "I feel very spoiled."

Chaz opens the champagne bottle. "You deserve the best, Taylor." He pours two glasses and hands me one.

I lift my glass. "To our last night in Paris, the most magical place I've ever been." Chaz smiles and we clink glasses.

For a while we just lean against the rail, drink our champagne and gaze out over the city. When the Eiffel Tower light show starts, I look down at my ring which sparkles just as much if not more. I don't want this trip to end, I realize. I'm not sure what has been real and what has been fake, but it all feels incredibly genuine to me. And I want it to stay that way.

I set my glass down and feel like dancing. The energy of the ballet still fills me, and I do a little turn, feeling Chaz watch.

"Are you going to show me some of your moves?" he asks in a teasing voice.

"I have quite a few," I say.

"Give me the basics. Like how you do those fancy turns."

"You mean pirouettes?" I ask with a laugh.

"Sure."

"I even brought my pointe shoes," I say. "I need more room, though." I head back into the suite and Chaz follows. He drops down on the couch and reclines on a pillow looking like some kind of lounging prince. His tie is gone and the first couple of buttons on his shirt are open and expose the tan column of his throat. He looks far too handsome and regal, especially with his smoothly shaven face.

I grab my shoes-- I don't go anywhere without them-- and tie the ribbons around my ankles. Then, I situate myself in the middle of the room. "To warm up my feet, I need to do a few relevés. That means raising myself up on my points." I get into position and go up onto my toes a few times. "Now, I get into fourth position, then relevé onto my front leg while bringing my back leg into passé and then bringing both of my arms into first position."

I hold the position and glance over at Chaz who watches me like he's mesmerized. "Next, I pick a spot on the wall to focus on while I'm turning. This is called spotting. Finally, you put it all together and get a pirouette." I do several in a row and my Chanel dress lifts and flows as I spin.

"Show me more," he says. "What's the one where you spin really fast?"

"Oh, a fouetté." I stop the tutorial and launch into a series of five fast fouettés, whipping around in circles. I don't stop and instead keep dancing, channeling all my emotions from the last two days into the choreography. I got engaged, attended the Paris Opera Ballet and gave my virginity to Chaz. It's been a whirlwind trip and one that I will never forget.

My only question is how much of it is true? Am I living in a make-believe world right now?

After I finish dancing, Chaz stands up and gives me a round of applause. "You're so fucking talented," he says. "It blows my mind that you can do all that."

"Thanks. I'll never be in the Paris Ballet Company, but I work really hard."

"You don't need the Paris Ballet Company," he says and pulls me into his arms. "You need to stay in Los Angeles with me."

When his mouth covers mine, I go up on my pointe shoes and wrap my arms around his neck. I kiss him back with everything I've got. Our kisses feel different tonight. Somehow more desperate, like we can't get enough of each other. He slides his hands down over my rear end and I jump up, wrapping my legs around his waist.

We devour each other and I slide my hands through his hair, down his hard arms and then around. As I start to fumble with the buttons on his shirt, he lifts his head. "Let me help you take your dress off before we ruin it."

He sets me down; unzips it and I slide it off and carefully hang it up. When I go to remove my pointe shoes, he shakes his head. "Leave them on," he murmurs as his gaze roams over my satin shoes then up to my pale pink bra and panties.

Heat swirls through my lower stomach and I watch Chaz shrug out of his white, button-down shirt. His bronze, muscular chest is a tempting sight and when he moves in, I reach out and run my hands over it. "I love touching you," I say in a low voice.

His gaze lowers, watching as my fingers explore each ridge. "I love watching you touch me."

I reach for his belt and unbuckle it. I'm feeling bolder and want to touch him in other places, too. I tug his zipper down and he chuckles. "Are you in a hurry tonight?"

I nod and shove his pants and boxer briefs down. When he springs free, I lower my hand and wrap my fingers around his hard length. His eyes slide shut, and he curses under his breath as I continue my exploration. I begin to move my hand up and down, gauging his response. "Like this?" I ask.

He groans. "Exactly like that." But, a minute later, he pulls my hand away. "You're going to make me come before I'm even inside you."

When he drops his head and kisses me hard, I lean into him. I feel his deft fingers unsnap my bra and as it slides forward, he's already pushing my panties down. Apparently, I'm not the only one in a hurry tonight. Then, he scoops me up and carries me over to the large bed.

I stretch out across the comforter, and he lays over me. When his warm, naked skin touches mine, it's like my entire body catches fire. Molten heat pours through me, angling straight down to the spot between my thighs and I want this man so much I ache.

As he leaves a trail of wet kisses down my neck and over my breasts, I writhe beneath him, unable to wait another minute. "Now, Chaz, please." I push up against him, desperate for him to be inside me, moving, possessing me.

I hear the crinkle of a foil packet and then he's there, hovering at my entrance, and I grab his face between my hands. "Do it," I say, and he instantly obeys. With one thrust, our gazes locked, he sinks into my body, and I cry out, arching up and completely open to him. And, not just my body, I realize. Also, my heart and soul. Maybe that's not a good thing but, right at this moment, I don't care.

His bright cobalt gaze sucks me deep and I can't look away as he begins a fast, hard rhythm. I lift my hips to meet each stroke, legs wrapping around him, pointe shoes arching, and together we go to some other level, some other place. When those clever fingers of his begin to caress me down low, massaging and swirling, I feel like I'm standing at the edge of a cliff, looking over, on the verge of jumping.

And, then I leap out into the air. The pleasure is intense, and the waves consume me. I call out his name, lost in the feel of our joined bodies, and it's like I'm floating high among the clouds. My head drops back on the pillow and above me, Chaz groans through his release then drops down beside me.

I feel dazed, still breathing hard, and look over at him. He's staring at me, a strange look on his handsome face. I reach my left hand out and lay it over his heart, feeling its strong, steady beat. Both our gazes drop to the sparkling diamond on my finger.

With every moment that passes, I'm becoming more and more invested. I hope his heart is where mine is right now. But I really have no idea and that's a very scary feeling.

Our whirlwind Parisian trip ends the next morning and we have an early flight back to Los Angeles. I can't lie-- I'm sad to go and wish we had more time. The flight back is long and quieter than the one out. It's like both of us are caught up in our thoughts and have no idea where we stand with each other now. But neither wants to ask and look vulnerable.

Chaz is still as kind, affectionate and considerate as ever. He holds my hand often throughout the flight, makes sure I have everything I need and gives me a little smile every so often.

I want this to be real. So badly.

The thought flits through my head and it's not the first time. Chaz Stone is everything I always wanted, and he makes me so happy. Happier than I have ever been. I wish I knew where we stood and what to expect when we land back in LA. But I'm too nervous to ask.

After landing and collecting our luggage, a car waits for us. The drive to Sunset Terrace is quiet and the closer we get, the more my nerves increase. When the car pulls up to the curb, Chaz helps me get my suitcase out and wheels it up the pathway for me.

In front of my door, I turn to him, unsure where we stand.

"Did you have a good time?" he asks.

"The best." I smile and wait for him to smile back. But, instead, he cups my face in his hands, leans down and kisses me thoroughly. Very reluctantly, we pull apart.

"Rest up and I'll call you later."

"Okay." I watch him begin to walk away and my heart stutters. "Chaz!"

He stops and turns back around, brow raised.

I'm not sure what possesses me to call out to him. I guess I just don't want to see him leave. "Merci. For everything," I say.

He gives me that bright-white smile. "You're welcome, Sugar Plum."

For a long moment, I can't move, and I watch him get into the car. After it drives away, I let out a pent-up breath and turn to unlock my door.

"Sugar Plum?"

I look over to see Morgan standing in her open door. *Oh, crap.*

"Was that *Chaz Stone?*"

"Yes," I admit.

Suddenly she squeals and runs up to me. "Is that an *engagement ring?*" She grabs my hand and lifts it up to admire the brilliant diamonds.

I nod and she screams. "Oh, my God, c'mon in before someone calls the cops because of all your screaming."

We head inside and I roll my suitcase out of the way. Morgan plops down on the couch cross-legged and watches me with wide, curious eyes. "I have two hours before I have to be at my other job and I want to hear every juicy detail," she says.

"Did Jasmine tell you anything?"

"Nothing. Probably because I haven't seen her."

"Probably," I agree and sit down next to her.

"Where were you?"

"We should probably start at the beginning," I say and then start to tell her about that night at Club Noir when Chaz first approached me. She listens intently, asks a question from time to time and when I finish up with Paris, her jaw hangs on the floor.

"I am speechless," she finally says. "First Savannah then Hailey and now you. Why don't these things ever happen to me?"

Her tone is light, and I know she's joking, but at the same time, she's not. Poor Morgan works constantly and puts her sick mother above everything else in her life-- her dream of becoming an actress, her social life and her romantic life. More than anyone, she needs a man like Chaz to sweep into her life and bring some light in to brighten the shadows.

But she's going to have to find her own man because Chaz is all mine.

"Paris sounds like it was amazing. In every way," she adds and smirks.

"It was a dream come true. God, Morgan, I like him so much."

"Are you falling in love with him?"

I frown and have tried very hard to avoid thinking about this exact question, but when Morgan brings up the "L" word, I know it's true. No point in denying it. "Yes," I whisper.

Morgan squeals and bounces up and down on the couch.

"I know our relationship isn't real, but nothing has ever felt so right."

"That ring sure looks real," Morgan says and lifts my hand up again. "Oh, good God, it's blinding!"

We both laugh. I let out a shaky, unsure breath and Morgan squeezes my hand.

"You have to follow your heart, Tay. It won't lead you astray."

"I'm just scared," I say. "He's an actor and used to putting on performances and playing different roles. What if that whole time in Paris, he was just pretending? It would break my heart."

"You have to stay positive."

I nod and give her a little smile. "Thanks, Morgan."

"And, when you guys get married, I expect to be invited to some cool Hollywood parties so I can find my man. If he even exists."

"He exists," I promise her. "It'll just probably be in the last place you'd expect."

After Morgan leaves, I step around my mountain of dirty laundry which has increased even more, take a shower and wash the plane ride off me. Clean and refreshed, I slip into a t-shirt and boxers and look in my fridge. Compared to the food I've been eating, this looks pathetic. But, I'm starving so I scrounge up a frozen pasta dinner and nuke it.

While I'm waiting for it to finish cooking, there's a knock on my door. I jump up, wondering who it could, secretly hoping it's Chaz. But, when I open the door, it's a guy around my age who I'm guessing is a courier when he hands me an envelope.

"Delivery for Miss Taylor Quinn," he says.

"That's me."

"Can you sign here?" He extends a clipboard and I pick up the pen and scrawl my signature across the line.

"Thanks," I say and open the manilla envelope. There's another envelope inside and I slide it out. My heart stops then speeds up like crazy when I spot the fancy emblem in the corner that belongs to the American Ballet Academy.

I unseal what can only be an invitation to audition and pull the card out. Tears fill my eyes, the words blurring. Chaz did exactly as he promised.

I'm going to audition for ABC, and I have never been happier.

Chapter Fourteen: Chaz

Since the moment I left Taylor earlier today, she has consumed my every thought. Flashes of Paris tease me, and I don't think I've ever had such a good time as I had with Taylor. The moment I get home, I call Lizette LaFleur, my good friend over at ABC. I rave about Taylor for probably 20 minutes straight before Lizette chuckles.

"You're in love," she says.

Love? The word throws me because I don't let myself go there. But now I wonder? Did I begin to fall for my little ballerina somewhere along the way? Somewhere, most likely, in Paris? Shit, I don't want to admit it, but I'm not going to lie to myself, either. Every moment I have spent with her has been precious.

Maybe it was when we slept together, and she gave me her virginity. Or, when I saw tears slip down her cheeks at the ballet. Or, quite possibly, it could've been when I woke up in the middle of the night with her body curved against mine and I listened to her soft, steady breathing and inhaled her peaches and cream scent. And, in that moment, I knew that no one has ever or will ever affect me so deeply or thoroughly as Taylor Ann Quinn.

I miss her and it's only been a few hours. I told her that I'd call her tonight so what the hell. I pick up my phone and hit her number. When she answers, my world tilts a bit. "Hey, Sugar Plum," I say, my voice husky. "How are you?"

"So good," she says. "I got the invite from ABC."

"Good. You deserve it."

"I'm going to practice until my feet bleed," she promises.

"I don't think that's necessary."

"I'm determined to make the company. I won't let myself or you down."

"I know and I have every faith in you."

"Tomorrow, I have classes and then I'm going over to the studio to practice. If you want, you could stop by later and watch."

"I'd like that," I say.

We talk for a few more minutes and then say goodnight. Taylor spent the last two nights in my bed and now that she's not here, I don't like it. I'm so close to jumping in my car and driving over to her place, but I know that I shouldn't. I feel like I'm getting too close, too emotionally involved and I need to keep my ass home tonight. I need to keep my distance even though I don't want it.

I sleep like shit because Taylor isn't in my bed. But the first thing I think when I wake up is that I'm going to see her tonight at the ballet studio. I feel like a kid on Christmas Eve, and I can't wait. The day drags, but when I get her text around 6pm, my heart soars.

I head out and drive over to the studio where she's practicing on Sunset Boulevard. It's after-hours and quiet when I walk inside. She told me she's at the end of the hall in the room on the left and when I get to the door, I push it open and walk inside.

Taylor is in the middle of dancing, and I freeze and watch her. Her grace and talent astound me. I've seen her do some fancy spins and turns, but now she's in full-performance mode, gliding across the floor and moving with the lightness, poise and elegance of a true professional.

She wears a baby-pink leotard with a matching sheer skirt and her red hair is pulled back in a low, tight bun. I can tell when she catches sight of me in the floor-to-ceiling mirror because a smile curves her lips. Lips that I can't wait to kiss.

After she finishes, I give her a slow round of applause as she walks over. "That was phenomenal," I tell her and pull her into my arms.

"You didn't even see the whole thing."

"Then, you're going to have to do it for me all over again." I press my forehead against hers and breathe her peachy scent into my nose.

"I'm all sweaty."

"I don't care." I grasp her hips and drop my mouth to capture hers. My tongue slides past her lips and she meets it with hers and the kiss morphs into hot need. It's been over 24 hours since I've seen her, and I can't get enough. It feels like it's been fucking forever. The overwhelming need to possess her, to mark her as mine, fills me and my hands slide over her ass and squeeze. I yank her against my erection to let her know just how much I want her.

"Chaz," she gasps.

I'm sucking the soft curve where her neck and throat meet, determined to give her a hickey for the whole world to see. *Mine.* No one else can have Taylor. I think a part of me is panicking a little because I know the clock is ticking and our time together is slipping away.

But I don't want to think about the stupid contract. Hell, I can't think straight at all as the hard-on of a lifetime surges against my zipper. All I can think about is how much I want this woman. *Now.*

When Taylor's hand unbuttons my pants and slips down into my boxers, I groan. Those delicate, graceful fingers release my aching cock and then she drops down in front of me.

Fuck. This is an unexpected surprise and one of the things I love about her. She's passionate, spontaneous and knows exactly how to touch me. I lean back against the wall and my gaze instantly goes to the mirror across from us. I stare at the back of her fiery red head as she strokes me and then I look down just as she looks up and takes me into her mouth.

The moment her lips wrap around my cock, I drop my head back and give in to the overwhelming sensations. Electricity shoots down my spine and my hips jut forward as she sucks me deep. My hands move to cup her head, but she needs no guidance, and I just savor the feel of her hot, wet mouth.

I can feel my control slipping and I can't hold out much longer. "I'm going to come," I warn her.

But she doesn't pull away, only sucks me deeper and I lose it. The orgasm hits me hard, and she swallows each spurt of my powerful release. My entire body rattles as though an earthquake rolls inside of it and I groan long and hard. *Christ, that was intense.*

Taylor stands up and I just look at her, knowing my eyes probably look a little glazed over. "Was that okay?" she whispers.

I pull her close and kiss her long and hard. When I drag my mouth away, she's looking up at me with inquisitive blue eyes. "Better than okay. Try mind-blowing."

"If you haven't noticed yet, I'm a perfectionist."

"Well, if you want to practice that more tonight, feel free." She smiles as I close my pants back up and all I want to do is get out of here and drop her in my bed so we can finish what we started.

"Are you about done here?" I ask. When she nods, I grab her hand and head for the exit.

"Wait," she says with a laugh. "I have to get my bag and change my shoes."

"Hurry up, baby," I tell her. "I've got plans for you tonight."

When we arrive back at my place, I am so hot for my little ballerina that we are barely inside the door before I lift her up, pin her to the wall and start to have my way with her. Just when my tongue is halfway down her throat, I hear voices and we both freeze.

"Shit," I swear.

Outside, my brother and John pause on the other side of the door as Brand unlocks it. As they walk in, I release Taylor and she slides down the front of my body.

"Hi, Taylor," Brand says with a cheeky grin.

She swallows hard and peers around my shoulder. "Hi, Brand."

"Well, well, well," John says and looks from Taylor's flushed face to me. "Hope we aren't interrupting anything."

"You're always interrupting, John."

"What can I say? My timing is impeccable."

"His timing is shit," I tell Taylor.

Suddenly, John whips out several magazines that he had tucked under his arm and out of sight. "Seems like you two are the new It-Couple."

I look over and see that an image of Taylor and I kissing in front of the Cartier store in Paris dominates each glossy cover. Then, John's eyes go wide as saucers when he sees the large diamond on her left hand which still lays on my shoulder. *Fuck, fuck, fuck.*

"You're *engaged?*" He looks stunned for a moment then walks over and slaps me on the back. "Holy shit, Stone. I don't know what to say."

"How about congratulations?" Brand suggests.

"Yeah, of course, congrats. Seems like you're moving pretty fast, but if you're happy-"

"I am," I say and start to pull Taylor out of the room and away from him before he says anything stupid. I have this nagging feeling that I'm about to dodge a bullet.

But nope. I get shot point blank.

"Who knew our little bet would've turned into an actual, full-blown relationship."

Fuck me.

Taylor gives him a funny look as Brand nudges John toward the kitchen to grab a couple of beers. On their way out, Brand gives me an apologetic look, but the damage has been done. I felt it the moment Taylor's body tensed against me.

"Bet?" she asks and moves away from me. "What is he talking about?"

"Nothing. He's crazy." When I reach for her hand, she yanks it back.

"Chaz, tell me."

At this moment, I want to murder John. We were so close to heading into my bedroom where we would've had hot sex all night long and now, I have to try to explain my way out of this. "Why don't we talk in my room?"

"Let's talk right here," she says, voice firm.

I let out a sigh. What else can I tell her except the truth? I won't lie to her. My ex-wife lied to me all the time and I refuse to do that to Taylor. I respect her way too much to make her look like a fool. "Remember the night we met at the club?"

"Of course."

"Well, I was having a really bad day. That's why we were there. The guys wanted to cheer me up after I didn't get the role I wanted."

"A film role?"

"The lead in some action movie. They wanted to give it to some young kid, and it pissed me off."

"And that's when you started thinking you should get a younger girlfriend?"

I nod. "To help boost my image."

"So, you approached me and hoped I would be your fake girlfriend?"

Here is where I should've just nodded and let her think she was right. But, no, I don't do that. Instead, I tell her the truth and make one of the biggest mistakes of my life.

"Not exactly."

"What do you mean?"

"The guys were razzing me all night about the role they did offer me." I grit my teeth then spill it. "They wanted me to play the lead's grandfather."

Other than the arch of one cinnamon-dusted brow, Taylor says nothing. She just waits for me to continue.

"And, like I said, I was mad and upset. Then, I saw you. I couldn't stop watching you and the guys noticed and started razzing me about it. And…" My voice trails off and every instinct is telling me to shut up.

"And?"

"And Ozzy made me a bet. That I had one week to sleep with you, or I had to accept the grandpa role."

Disbelief flashes through her eyes. "I was a *bet?*"

The hurt in her voice is like a punch in my gut. "At first. But then I got to know you and-"

Taylor throws her hands up. "I can't believe this. So, the only reason you approached me is because you bet your friends that you could fuck me?"

"No, I mean yes. But it became more than that."

"Yeah, then you got the bright idea to have me sign a contract to clean up your old-ass image. And I was stupid enough to do it."

Anger spikes through me like a hot poker and my eyes narrow. "You signed it willingly so don't act like I forced you to do anything you didn't want to do."

"That's not the point!" Her voice is getting louder and I'm sure my brother and John are getting an earful.

"Lower your voice," I hiss.

"Why? Everyone knows this is fake."

"No, they don't. Only Brand knows about the contract. And Lang."

"Oh, great!" she snaps.

"Well, he wrote the damn thing."

"You really are too much!"

"What's that supposed to mean?"

"You dangled the one thing I wanted more than anything in my face, knowing I wouldn't be able to say no, and then used me."

"I didn't use you. Not really."

Her blue eyes cloud over. "You took my virginity, Chaz. I thought-" Her voice abruptly cuts off and she looks down at the ring on her finger. Then, she twists it off and shoves it against my chest. "Congratulations. Looks like you won your fucking bet."

I grab the ring before it can fall and hold it out. "Put it back on. You signed a contract. You're my fiancée until we decide this is over."

"Oh, it's over."

"No, it isn't. Just because you got your audition doesn't mean you can walk away. I didn't get my role yet."

She sucks in a sharp breath. "I'm done."

"We have a legally-binding agreement. Break it and I will sue you." *Okay, not really, but I had to threaten her.*

"You're an asshole."

"Tell me something I don't know."

"I have nothing else to say to you." Taylor spins away and stomps over to the front door. She throws it open, and I grab her arm.

"You can't leave," I say. But, in my head, I'm thinking: *You can't leave me.*

"Yes, I can," she says and jerks her arm out of my grip. Anger flashes in her blue eyes. "Don't call me or text me or expect me to be at your beck and call anymore."

White hot anger fills me. "So, you're breaking the contract?"

She lets out a frustrated sigh. "Screw your contract! And screw you, Chaz. Find some other naive girl to pay to be your girlfriend. I'm done."

Then, she marches out and I stand there by myself and look down at the ring in my palm. *Shit.* My eyes slip closed, and I know that I just fucked up royally.

Chapter Fifteen: Taylor

I hold it together pretty well until I get back to my apartment. Then, something inside me fractures. I think it's my heart. Dropping down on the couch, I sob my eyes out.

How could he?

I've never felt so used in my life. Chaz never liked me or wanted to get to know me. The only reason he came up to me in the first place is because his stupid friend bet him that he couldn't get me into bed within a week. *Well, mission accomplished, Chaz. Congratulations.*

I feel like a fool and so completely confused. Was everything that happened a lie? More so than I even realized.

Was Paris a lie? I wonder.

The last three days in Paris were the best of my life. And now, it all seems like a joke. A very cruel joke that Fate played on me for agreeing to that stupid contract. I am so mad at Chaz right now but, really, I suppose that I am just as much to blame.

The bet pisses me off, but I feel my emotions spinning and the anger is morphing into sadness. I have no idea where we stand. I told him that I'm done, and I can't believe he threatened to sue me. Seriously? *Let him,* I think. If he wins, the only thing he'll get from me is a big-ass, dirty pile of laundry.

Apparently, he wants to keep the charade up, but my poor heart can't take it. How in the world would I go to events with him, laugh with him and kiss him, knowing it's not real after what we shared? *Impossible.* I would shatter. With tears still streaming down my face, I wander down to the bathroom and hope that a shower will help.

It doesn't.

I need my mind to shut down, so I crawl into bed, praying for sleep. *Yeah, right.* Instead, I toss and turn for the next few hours, thoughts of Chaz keeping me awake. When I finally drift off, he comes to me in my dreams. And we're back in Paris.

Everything is beautiful and bright for a brief moment. And then I wake up. Alone. I've gotten used to cuddling up to Chaz's big, warm body and now my bed feels cold and empty. It's early, still dark out, but I know I won't be able to fall back asleep. So, instead, I drag myself out of bed, use the bathroom, throw a fresh leotard on and pin my hair back.

Even though it's a Sunday, I'm going to go over to the studio and practice. I'm going to spin and twirl until my feet feel like they're going to fall off. The audition for ABC is the one really good thing that I have left, that I'm clinging to like a lifeline right now, and I can't mess it up. I need to walk in there next week and own it. I must make the company because if I don't then everything will have been in vain.

It's also the beginning of the new month and I remember that I owe Ryan Fox a rent check. I sigh and start filling out a blank check, hoping that I have enough in there to cover it. *Wait a minute*. I grab my phone and sign onto my bank account. *Holy shit*. The balance that stares back at me makes my jaw drop. Surely that can't be right.

Chaz agreed to deposit two-thousand dollars in my account each week and that's what I'm expecting to see. Not ten times that. Is he crazy? *Why did he put all that extra money in here?* I wonder. I have no idea, but I can't think about it right now. I must focus and go dance.

I grab my bag and stop by Ryan and Hailey's corner apartment. I tuck the check in the mail slot and imagine them sound asleep right now, wrapped up in each other's arms. They're so very lucky.

This is why I should've said no to his stupid agreement. My mind is all over the place when it should be laser-focused on the upcoming audition. I've never felt so lost.

The studio isn't far away, and I decide to walk over. I punch in the code to let myself in and walk down to the end of the hall and switch the light on. When my eyes hit the floor-to-ceiling mirror across the way, I instantly remember the other night. When Chaz leaned against the wall, and I dropped down to my knees and sucked him until he came down my throat.

I hadn't ever done that before, but his response was a pretty good indication that I not only did it right, but also a pretty damn good job. With a sigh, I drop my bag and begin to stretch. It's going to be a long day and I don't plan on leaving until I'm on the verge of collapse.

I practice hard, probably sweat off five pounds and hydrate often. Around four o'clock in the afternoon, I'm spent and decide I should probably leave before I do something stupid like push too hard and hurt myself.

As I walk back to Sunset Terrace, thoughts of Chaz fill my head. I try to ignore them and when I walk up the pathway, I hear laughter and voices. I totally forgot it's the weekly Sunday barbecue and all the neighbors are out by the pool, catching up. The smell of hotdogs and burgers on the grill fill the air and I see Ryan cooking them. Hailey and Jasmine sit on lounge chairs next to the pool, deep in gossip, and Mason and Cody, my upstairs neighbors who are pro-surfers, splash around in the pool.

I am not in the mood to be social but, as soon as they see me, the girls wave.

"Taylor!" Jasmine calls. "Come here."

I grit my teeth and try not to sigh. Instead, I paste a smile on my face and walk over.

"Were you practicing today?" Hailey asks.

"It's Sunday!" Jasmine exclaims. "And Sunday is a day of rest."

"I didn't do much resting today. I've been at the studio since 5am."

"Why?"

I let my bag slide off my shoulder and sit down on the nearest lounge chair. "I just got invited to audition for the American Ballet Company."

Jasmine gives me a knowing smile and Hailey's eyes go wide.

"Congratulations, Taylor! That's amazing. I thought you said you didn't know anyone over there."

"Well, I didn't, but I just met someone who helped me get the audition."

"That's so great," Hailey gushes.

"Yeah," I say without much enthusiasm. It's obvious by my expression and tone that I am far from happy.

"Are you okay?" Jasmine asks, eyeing me closely. "And, where have you been the last few days? The mailman left a box over at my place for you."

It's the absolute last thing I want to happen, but I feel my eyes fill with tears. "I was in Paris," I say and start to cry.

"Oh, my God, honey, what's wrong?" Jasmine slides off her chair, sits down next to me and wraps an arm around my shoulders. "You signed it?" she asks in a low voice.

I nod and sniffle. As I swipe the tears away, I glance over at Hailey and see her confused concern. "It's a long story. But basically, I think I fell in love with someone who doesn't want me."

Hot tears scald my eyes all over again and Jasmine pulls me into a hug. "Don't cry, sweetie. If he doesn't realize how amazing you are, then he's an idiot."

"How did I miss all this?" Hailey asks, completely baffled...

Jasmine gives her a sidelong glance. "You're so wrapped up in Foxy Flyboy over there, I don't think you'd notice an earthquake."

Hailey looks over at Ryan, a dreamy expression on her face. "He does keep me rather...busy."

Jasmine gives a snort and lets me go. "What can we do, Tay?"

"Nothing," I say, absolutely miserable.

"So, he took you to Paris?"

I let out a long, shaky sigh and spill it. Hailey has no idea what's going on, so I start from the beginning and tell her how Chaz approached me at Club Noir. And, this time, I add the part about the bet.

Jasmine's dark, almond-shaped eyes narrow. "Why are men so damn childish? I mean, c'mon."

"So, the bet led to the contract, and he lured you in with the promise of securing you an audition for ABC," Hailey summarizes.

I nod. "Am I stupid?"

"No," they both say at once.

"I feel like such an idiot. And he put on a damn good show. I really thought he cared. And the last couple of days in Paris were magical. At least to me."

Jasmine rubs a hand on my back shoulder. "None of this is your fault. It sounds like Chaz Stone is in the middle of a mid-life crisis and he's dragging you down with him."

Hailey sits up straighter. "Chaz Stone? *The actor?*"

"I guess I left that part out."

"That's a pretty big part not to mention. He's so handsome. Did you see that movie where he robs the Vegas casino?"

"Hailey," Jasmine says in a warning voice.

"Sorry. It was only okay," she adds quickly.

"Last time we talked; you were reluctant to get involved with all this. And now you think you're in love?"

"I know it sounds silly, but he was really sweet to me. I've never had anyone dote on me like he did. He opened doors, fed me, bought me presents, made sure I was taken care of-- and, as nice as all that was, it was more about the way he made me feel. Like I was the only woman in the room."

"Oh, Lord. That's how they get you. They make you feel special."

"He has this way of looking at me that makes my heart stop then start up again really fast. It's like he's looking right into my very soul." I look down at my legs and pick a piece of lint off my leotard. "We slept together."

I notice Jazz and Hailey exchange a look. "And?" Jazz asks.

"It was sooo good."

They both give me little smiles. "Our little ballerina is a woman," Jazz says.

I roll my eyes. "He was so considerate and gentle. I never imagined it would be so amazing."

"It's so amazing because you have feelings for him," Jasmine says.

"Strong feelings," Hailey adds.

"I'm pretty sure that I fell in love with him. Last night, after I found out about the bet, I was so mad. I felt used and had to remind myself that everything was a lie and the only reason we were together was because we signed a contract."

"Did he at least apologize?" Hailey asks.

"He threatened to sue me."

"*What?*" they both cry.

"He said I can't walk away and, if I do, then it's a breach of our agreement."

"What a dick," Jasmine says.

"He's right, though. I agreed to a fake relationship."

"What are you going to do?" Hailey asks.

I shrug. "If I see it through, I can't cross that line again. I'm a means to an end. He's made that pretty clear."

"He should've known better," Jazz says.

"Maybe it's like with me and Ryan. Sometimes the age difference freaks them out."

But I shake my head. "No. He wanted a younger woman on his arm. I think maybe I was just a game or a challenge. In the end, he's this huge star and I'm nobody."

"Don't say that" Jasmine says. "You're going to be a prima ballerina."

"Not if I don't make a company." I feel tears threaten again. "San Diego and San Francisco didn't want me. So, why in the world would ABC? They're one of the most prestigious companies in the entire country."

"Because you're so fucking talented," Jazz says. "Don't doubt yourself. You've worked too hard and practiced your entire life to get to this point. If you let some man distract you when you need to focus, I'm going to kill you."

Hailey nods. "You're right on the verge of your dream, Taylor. You can't give up now."

I know they're right. "I won't," I whisper.

"You're damn right you won't," Jasmine says.

Hailey and Jasmine hug me. "You've got this," Hailey assures me.

I wish I felt as confident in myself as they did.

Everyone knows something is wrong and I can feel the curious looks from Mason, Cody and Ryan. When the girls and I stop talking, Ryan announces that the food is ready. Mason and Cody get out of the pool and fill their plate while Ryan comes over and hands me a hotdog and some chips.

"You okay?" he asks.

I force a nod.

"You need me to beat anyone up for you?"

I feel a smile tug at my lips. "I'll let you know," I say, and he pats my back. Even though I'm not hungry, I make myself eat. I must keep my strength up and push Chaz to the back of my mind. The girls are right-- this is too important to blow, and all my attention needs to be on staying strong and acing this audition.

The mood isn't as cheerful and carefree as it usually is at our Sunday barbecues, and I feel bad. I know I'm bringing the energy down so as soon as I finish eating, I say goodbye and get up to leave.

"Hey," Cody says and follows me.

I glance over and he gives me a smile.

"If you need me or Mase to kick someone's ass, just let us know, okay?" I look over at Mason and he lifts his chin to let me know he's got my back.

"Thanks, Cody. I appreciate it."

I love how the men here have my back. I only wish Chaz did, too.

Back in my apartment, I sit down and massage my sore feet. I really put them through the wringer today. I have blisters everywhere, but I must dance again tomorrow so all I can do is soak my feet in some warm water and hope they feel better by morning.

When I reach for my phone, I see a missed call and text from Chaz. My heart beats faster as I slide the bar over and read his text: *We need to talk. Call me.*

He's so bossy and his outright command makes me not want to talk to him. I take a deep breath and listen to his message. "Taylor, ignoring me isn't going to improve the situation. Let's figure this out. Please, call me."

His deep voice does something funny to my traitorous insides and I don't think talking to him right now is the best thing for me. The girls told me to focus on myself and my audition and that's exactly what I'm going to do.

I turn my phone off and dry my poor, aching feet.

After the audition, I'll worry about Chaz. In the meantime, it's best to pretend that he doesn't even exist.

Chapter Sixteen: Chaz

I can't believe she hasn't called or texted me back. It's been almost a week and I'm beyond angry. With an annoyed huff, I swipe my phone up and hit her number again. It goes straight to voicemail.

"Fuck." I hurl the phone into a couch cushion. I have a benefit to attend tonight, and my new fiancée should be on my arm. I suppose I could go over to her place and remind her that she agreed to be available and go to this stuff, but I know it would just cause a wicked fight.

All because of that stupid, goddamn bet.

I guess it was time for us to both wake up, though. Paris was a beautiful distraction and we both briefly forgot that our relationship was fake. I'm not sure when it exactly happened, but things went too far, and feelings became involved.

It never should've happened. I shouldn't have slept with her, for one. Huge mistake. Being innocent and untried, she developed expectations and apparently feelings for me.

But didn't I do the same?

Fuck. This is the most confusing situation, and I must keep my heart out of it. But the truth is, Taylor sucked me into her world and now that she's gone, I feel lost. I'm unhappy, annoyed, frustrated and lonely. *So damn lonely.*

I pour more whiskey into my glass and take a long sip. Then, I grab my phone and open it up to the pictures of us beneath the arch of the Eiffel Tower. For a long time, I look at the one where we're kissing.

The truth is I miss my little ballerina and I don't know if what we experienced in Paris was real or just an illusion. Since Sabrina, I've had no desire for a serious relationship, and I certainly am not capable of falling in love in a week. It's ludicrous.

Yes, we had great sex and, sure, whenever I think about Taylor my heart kicks up a notch. It's only lust, though, right?

And, okay, maybe I want to see her, and I even feel this strange urge to take care of her. That's why I deposited some extra money in her account. I don't want her eating frozen dinners and running out of quarters for laundry. I made a promise to take care of her. Sure, maybe twenty grand was a little much but it's important to me that she can get what she needs and not stress about finances.

Maybe I'm turning soft in my old age. No, that's not it. I like watching over her, protecting her, acting like a Daddy-figure. Just like I said I would.

When my phone rings, I dive for it, hoping to see Taylor's name on the screen. Instead, it's only my agent and I frown. "Hey, Cal."

"Chaz, how are you? Were you going to tell me about your hot, new fiancée or just make me read about it in the magazines like every other peasant?"

"I think you just answered your own question," I say in a dry voice.

"Funny, Chaz. Seriously, though, those pics out of Paris with your new babe stirred up some serious interest. I've got two reputable magazines and four television shows who want to interview you."

I could care less about interviews. "What about that action movie?"

He goes quiet.

"Do they want me for the lead?" I ask.

Cal clears his throat. "I'm working on it. But I think this whole younger girlfriend thing is definitely going to help."

"Well, go work a little harder, Cal, and then call me back when the studio is ready to offer me the lead." I hang up and roll my eyes. *Fucking useless agents.* Hollywood is full of them and unless they're collecting their ten percent, they aren't good for much else.

I wish I could skip this benefit tonight, but the charity is for a good cause, and I promised the founder I'd be there. Even though I'm not in a mingling mood, I suppose I can make an appearance, stand in the corner for a while and drink until I can sneak out.

I put on my Gucci tuxedo, bow tie and dress shoes and slick my hair back with some mousse. I should shave, but really, who cares? Instead, I just splash some cologne on and leave. The driver takes me to a private country club in Calabasas and the first thing I do is go up to the bar and get a drink. I need to fortify myself with alcohol to get through the night ahead and help me forget about-

Fuck me. My gaze lands on my ex-wife and just when I thought the night couldn't get any worse, it turns into an absolute nightmare. As Sabrina Destin air-kisses someone's cheeks, her light gray eyes turn in my direction. I feel a sick rolling in my stomach and turn around. She is the last person I want to see right now. Or, ever, for that matter.

But Sabrina loves to be a pain in my ass so it isn't long before I smell her cloying rose scent right before she moves up beside me. "Hello, Chaz," she says in that deep, throaty voice of hers.

I take a drink then glance over at her. "Sabrina."

She eyes me with that silvery gaze of hers and I feel it run up and down me, cold and appraising. "What did you do to your hair? You look like a 1930s gangster."

I know it's not a compliment and I ignore it. "What do you want?"

"Just thought I'd say hi and see how you've been. No need to get riled up."

"I'm not getting-" I suck in a breath and finish my drink. Sabrina Destin has this way of getting under my skin and it needs to stop. I stopped loving her a long time ago so she shouldn't affect me any longer.

I set my empty glass down and turn my full attention to her. "I may look like a gangster, but you look lovely, as always." I'm determined to be an adult and not fall for her insults.

Her red lips curl up in a smile that doesn't reach her eyes. "All by yourself tonight?" she asks and glances around.

"That's right."

"Where's your fiancée? I was hoping to meet her."

I can hear the cutting tone in her voice and know a nasty comment is forthcoming. "She couldn't make it."

"Oh, that's too bad. I have a friend who needs a new babysitter and wanted to ask if she'd be interested."

"She isn't a babysitter," I say through gritted teeth. "She's a ballerina."

A thin, dark brow arches and I can tell Sabrina didn't expect that. No, she figures I'm with some floozy, child-bride who is only with me because she wants to be an actress or get her claws into a Sugar Daddy.

"She's extremely talented," I find myself saying and feel a swell of pride. "Taylor is practicing because she has a big audition coming up and I have every reason to believe that she's going to be part of a very prestigious company soon."

Sabrina gives a sniff of dismay. "Hmm. Well, she looks far too young for you. The two of you together look rather foolish. Or at least you do. Like an old man trying to reclaim his youth."

I expect her barbed words to make me angry, but I feel nothing. For the first time, Sabrina's nasty words have no effect and I smile. It feels damn good. "Whatever you say, Sabrina. Have a good evening."

The fact that I can walk away with a smile on my face annoys the shit out of her. I can tell when she purses her lips and then crosses her arms. It occurs to me that Sabrina and Taylor couldn't be any more different. While Sabrina is snarky and petty, Taylor is kind and noble with a heart that's wide-open.

For the first time, I begin to fully understand why I've avoided anything serious since my divorce. Sabrina crushed my heart and trust with her infidelity. Afterwards, I had nothing to offer anyone and no desire to be hurt again. But somehow Taylor helped put the broken pieces back together. She made me realize that it's okay to try again and take a chance.

Taylor showed me that a life without love is no way to live.

Holy. Shit.

I am in love with Taylor Quinn. Like massively, deeply, head-over-heels, and I can't live without her. *How can it be possible?* I barely know her. Actually, that's not true. I know the important things like how dedicated and loyal she is, and I know her dreams, her likes and dislikes. I know that she puts her heart and soul into her dancing and that if she doesn't get into ABC, she will feel like she somehow let me down because I called in a favor. I know how her eyes light up when she's happy. I know how sweet she tastes and every curve of her lithe body. I know the husky sounds she makes when I'm deep inside her.

Most of all, I know I can't tell her these things and that I hurt her. I feel like all I've managed to do is upset and distract her. And all that's going to do is make her lose focus. I can't fuck this audition up for her. The best thing I can do is give her space and let her achieve her dream. Then, if she's willing to talk to me…

No. It's becoming more and more clear to me that I'm a huge distraction. That I don't fit into her world. She has goals and dreams and the last thing I want to do is get in the way. Taylor will make ABC, or another company and she won't have time for me. She will have to focus on dancing, and I don't want to be the nag who keeps texting and calling and wondering when she can make time for me.

But the idea of never seeing Taylor again kills me.

"Chaz!"

I snap out of my reverie and look over to see Lizette LaFleur, my friend and Director of the American Ballet Academy. She's small with dark hair streaked with silver and a bright smile. "Lizette, so good to see you."

We hug and then I thank her for extending Taylor an invitation to audition. "She's absolutely amazing, Lizette. I've never seen anyone spin and whirl like her. It's as though her feet don't even touch the ground. It's otherworldly."

"When did you become such a ballet fan?"

"In all honesty, I guess I'd say I'm a Taylor fan. We attended the Paris Opera Ballet this past weekend and she told me they're the best of the best. But I'm telling you that she's just as good if not better."

"Well, then I'm very much looking forward to her audition tomorrow."

"It's tomorrow?"

Lizette frowns. "She didn't tell you?"

"Yes. I mean, I knew she got the invitation, but I didn't realize it was so soon."

"Why don't you come watch?"

I hesitate. "I'd like to, but…"

"But, what?"

"I don't want her to see me and get nervous."

"Is that the only reason?"

Damn, Lizette is perceptive. "And, also, because we…well, we ended our relationship."

"I'm sorry to hear that, Chaz. You sound so happy when you talk about her."

"Yeah, well, I messed things up like an idiot."

She touches my shoulder and gives me a small smile. "That doesn't mean it's over. Have you tried to work things out?"

"It's probably best if I give her space right now. The last thing I want to do is distract her. She's worked too hard and for too long to lose her dream because of me. I'd never forgive myself if I was the reason she messed up."

"Well, if she's as good as you say, then she has a very good chance of making it, right?"

"I'm not going to pretend I know anything about ballet, Lizette, but I do know how I feel. And, when Taylor dances, she has this way of making you feel the music, the emotions, the story."

"That can't be taught."

"No, I didn't think so."

"Come to the studio tomorrow. There's a private viewing room of the dance floor where you can watch her audition, but she won't be able to see you."

I frown. As much as I'd love to be there and support her, if by chance she saw me, it could be devastating. "I don't know," I say.

"Maybe she'll feel you just as much as you feel her. And, that support could make a world of difference. Think about it and let me know."

"Thanks, Lizette."

After I say hello to the charity's founder and bid a ridiculous amount on an auction item that I don't want, I leave. I don't know what to do about my feelings and the longing I feel for Taylor. It's killing me to think that she's mad at me. Maybe I should try to call her again.

No. I can't be a distraction. Not the night before her big audition. But, fuck, I don't want her to think I don't care. Because I do. So damn much.

After a shower and another glass of whiskey, I pick up my phone and put a text together that wishes Taylor good luck. My finger hovers over the send button, but I end up deleting it instead. I lean back and write another message.

And delete it. I do this about 20 more times but can't find the nerve to hit send. I feel like a lovelorn fool. A pathetic jerk who ruined the best thing that ever happened to him.

And now there's no getting her back. The sooner I can accept it, the better. Taylor is too good for me, and I refuse to bring her down. I'm a washed-up, aging actor who's divorced and obviously unable to have a real relationship.

I finish my drink, toss my phone away and tell myself for the thousandth time to leave Taylor alone.

I've done enough damage.

Chapter Seventeen: Taylor

I have literally done everything in my power to prepare for tomorrow's audition at the American Ballet Academy. From endless practices to stretching to breathing exercises to positive thinking, I know that I am finally ready. And nothing is going to distract me.

I've pushed thoughts of Chaz away. For now, at least. Other than ballet, I haven't let any other thoughts intrude. Concentration is key. Focus is necessary. And contact with Chaz could be my undoing.

Because I've fallen for the idiot.

No doubt about that now. This past week without him has been hell. But he doesn't love me. To him, I'm merely a means to an end. A way to boost his image and jumpstart his career.

When my phone beeps, I consider ignoring it, but it's probably my parents wishing me good luck. We spoke earlier and they're so proud of me. It makes me feel good and they're just another reason why I'm so determined to make the company.

I roll across my bed and reach for my phone. It's Jazz and her text is a string of emojis that make me laugh-- a dancing girl, champagne, flowers, a star, a four-leaf clover and the number one. *You've got this!* she writes with ten exclamation points. I tell her thank you and my phone beeps again and again and again.

All of a sudden, the texts pour in, all from my Sunset Terrace neighbors. Hailey, Ryan, Morgan, Mason, Cody, even Savannah who moved out a few months ago, all telling me to break a leg. My heart swells and I can feel their love and support. It means the world to me.

My goal, my dream, is a mere breath away and it's crucial that I don't slip up. These last couple of days, I've been pushing myself to my limits, throwing myself into long, brutal practices and now is my chance. My time to prove it to myself and everyone else that I can do this. I can achieve my dream.

The thing is the only reason I have this audition in the first place is because of Chaz. He believed in me maybe more than anyone else and encouraged me from the start to pursue my dream. Without him, tomorrow wouldn't even be happening.

I shake my head, trying to clear it. I can't do this right now. Can't think about him. As grateful as I am for this opportunity, I need to keep my eyes on the prize.

With positive thoughts in my head, I crawl beneath my covers and practice even in my dreams. I'm going to kick ass tomorrow and dance my tutu off to get into that company. And, only after my audition, will I allow myself to think about anything else.

The next day, I take extra time choosing my light pink leotard with its small, flowy skirt and I pull my red hair back in a low, tight bun that is all business. Other than mascara, I keep my makeup light and natural-looking. I know how the choreographers and directors of these companies prefer a simple look. Their focus will be on my physique and technique, and I can't distract them with anything else.

Yet, I also need to stand out. I won't be the only one there who was invited to audition and, in the beginning, it's a little like a cattle call. They will start us at the barre and quickly whittle us down to a mere handful...

I place my pointe shoes in my bag along with a few other things and head out. I feel like I'm doing a pretty good job controlling my nerves until I step out of the Uber and look up at the imposing brick building and sign above the door that reads American Ballet Company.

I take a deep breath, push through the door and check in at the desk. The receptionist gives me a number to pin on my leotard then tells me where to go. I walk down a long hallway, past dozens of dancers with numbers pinned to their leotards who nervously stretch and wait for the try outs to begin. I find a spot to sit down on the floor, change into my pointe shoes and start stretching.

There's no point in sizing up the competition, but there are probably about 50 of us. I have no idea what they're looking for and even the most talented dancer here may get cut because he or she isn't a perfect fit for the company at this time.

I just need to show off how strong my technique is and give them a taste of my personality.

You're going to make it, I tell myself. *They're going to love you.*

When the main studio door opens 20 minutes later, I look up and a woman stands there with a clipboard in her hand. "Hello and thank you for coming today. My name is Adeline Mosier, and I am the Artistic Director here at ABC. This year we're looking for about three women and two men to join the company. But that may change after we see you perform."

I feel the tension rise around me but tune it out.

"For today's audition, we will begin with barre work and from there you will either progress to centre floor combinations or not. Then, we will choose a handful of people to interview. Most of you will be cut, but please don't take it personally. It's not about you, but about what we're specifically looking for. There are certain requirements we need to fulfil, such as height, so that we have a unified aesthetic. That said, some requirements can change a bit from year to year, depending on the makeup of the company and the position we're looking to fill."

Adeline's gaze moves over each dancer, already judging us. "The position for which we are considering the dancer also affects the qualities we look for. Our repertory requires that every dancer in the company dances a lot, so a strong, well-rounded technique is imperative. You must also be musical and able to move quickly. With that said, please follow me and line up at the barre."

As we head into the studio, my gaze falls on a table where I instantly recognize Lizette LaFleur, the Director of the company, and another man who I'm guessing is the Assistant Director.

I smile at them then position myself at the barre, within their sight, and the audition begins as Adeline leads us through multiple exercises. The movements are all second nature to me and I flow through them effortlessly.

I try not to think too hard about how the three of them scrutinize my feet, leg extension, musicality and speed, among other qualities. I'm not sure how it's even possible, but the tension in the room increases and then the cuts begin.

In less than 30 minutes, 20 dancers are asked to leave. But I'm still here and, as our work ends at the barre, I turn around and a smile tugs at my lips.

The next part involves learning original choreography and then improvisation. It's probably the most nerve-wracking part, especially for the more inexperienced dancers, but I'm not overly worried. I love improv and it's what I do every night when I dance over at Club Noir.

I pick up the moves they teach us right away and with ease. We perform in groups of four or five and, when it's my turn, I make sure I am front, and centre and we flow through the dance. Out of my four, half of us get cut. But I make it through to the improv part and wait for the other groups to finish.

By this point, we've been dancing for hours, and the group has gone from 50 or so down to 15. I'm still feeling good and I'm third in line to show off my improv skills. I watch the other dancers ahead of me and they're good but seem a little stiff which I'm sure is nerves. I think the reason I'm not nervous right now is because I love dancing so much that it's like breathing. It's just who I am and what I do. I don't get nervous when I breathe so why would I get nervous when I dance?

Before I know it, it's my turn and I hustle over to face the table. The music plays and I take the choreography they just taught us and give it a new spin. I add some fancy jumps, extra spins and just feel the moves, letting them flow through me.

After I finish, I give Lizette, Adeline and the Assistant Director bright smiles. I am in my element and, at this moment, everything feels as it should.

Very, very right. ABC feels like it could really be my home and that's exciting. I just hope they feel the same way about me.

After this section of the audition, they cut ten dancers which leaves me and four others to be interviewed-- four girls and one guy.

Here's the part where my nerves kick up a notch. So far, they like my dancing. Now, let's just hope they like my personality.

They inform us of the interview order and I'm last. I head back out into the hall, slide down the wall and sit on the floor. I open my bag and take a big gulp of water. I've been through this twice before, made it all the way to the end and then received a rejection letter.

But today is going to be different. I can feel it.

I hear my phone vibrate in the side pocket and normally I'd ignore it. But, for some reason, I have the urge to look so I slip it out.

My stomach drops when I see Chaz's name on the screen, and I hesitate. Should I read it? My eyes slide shut, and I slide the bar over: *Good luck. I'm pulling for you and wish you nothing but the best and for all your dreams to come true. You've got this, Sugar Plum.*

Tears fill my eyes, but for the first time in a week, they aren't sad tears. Something in the message gives me hope and it also feels really good to know that he's thinking about me right at this very moment. Does he miss me? Am I more than just a contract to him? More than just a fake fiancée?

I have no idea.

"Taylor?" I look up and see Adeline. "We're ready for you."

I nod and stand up. But, first, I quickly respond to his text with the fairy emoji, slip my phone back in my bag and head back inside.

A chair sits in front of the table facing Lizette, Adeline and Mark, the Assistant Director. I take a seat and thank them for having me. They talk a little about the company and how they look for new dancers who would be a good fit, at every level from apprentice to principal.

"And, even if we don't bring you on this year, we might in the near future as we expand," Mark says.

Not what I want to hear.

They ask me about my dancing goals, and I tell them how I want to ultimately be a principal.

"Principals have to be the strongest," Adeline says, and I nod. "They should have some outstanding qualities that we can build on in their solo variations. They also need some extra magnetism to their presence because they have to hold every eye in the room."

"They dance the broadest range of difficult steps and their technique in all areas has to be excellent," Mark adds.

Lizette looks me over carefully and I wonder what she thinks is going on with me and Chaz. Did he tell her anything about our relationship? "Principals must also possess a highly refined musicality, which makes them entertain to watch over longer periods. It all boils down to that certain je ne sais quoi. Do you believe you have that, Taylor?" Lizette asks me.

I hope this isn't some sort of trick question designed to trip me up. "I can be humble, even a little shy sometimes," I say. "Trust me, no one blushes like I do. But, when it comes to dance, I leave my insecurities at the door. I'm confident and I do believe I have something special to offer when I step onto the floor, but that doesn't mean I don't work hard. Ballet is my life, and I will put the blood, sweat and tears into it to be the absolute best I can be. I don't think that ever stops because there's always something to learn or work on and improve. I always strive for perfection and will continue to do so. Even if I become a Prima Ballerina one day."

I'm not going to lie, they're a difficult group to read, but I know that I gave this audition my all. If they decide to choose someone else over me it's not because I messed up. It's simply because I didn't fulfil their current needs.

I feel really good and very proud of myself as I thank them for their time and walk out of the room. I did absolutely everything I could've done and now my fate lies in their hands. As I head toward the front door, my hand moves over the number pinned to my leotard. I think that everyone would be proud of me-- my family, my friends and, especially, Chaz. Hell, I'm proud of myself.

"Taylor?"

I stop and turn around, my eyes widening as Lizette walks up to me. Oh, my God, I suddenly get more nervous than I've been all day. "Hi," I say.

"I just wanted to come over and personally introduce myself." She offers me her hand and I shake it. "Any friend of Chaz's is a friend of mine."

"Auditioning for you today was an absolute honor," I say. "No matter what happens. And Chaz is-" My voice cuts off and all I can do is smile. "Well, I'm not sure what he said about me, but he's the best man I know."

Shit. I said it.

"I saw him the other night and he couldn't stop raving about you."

"The other night?"

She gives me a small, conspiratorial smile. "It's quite easy to see that he cares for you a great deal."

He does?

Her words take me by surprise, but could they be true? Why would he say anything good about me after our fight? I've been ignoring his calls and texts, until just now, anyway. I reneged on our contract. I even practically threw the engagement ring in his face.

Maybe he was just putting on a show for her, I tell myself.

Lizette reaches out and squeezes my arm. "For what it's worth, you knocked it out of the park today." She starts to walk away, leaving me dumbfounded. Then, she glances over her shoulder. "Make sure to tell Chaz I said hello."

I have no words, so I only nod. Once I'm outside, I squeal and do a flawless jeté, leaping through the air like a gazelle.

Chapter Eighteen: Chaz

All day, I sit inside the small, cramped viewing room with the tinted window, on the edge of my seat, and watch Taylor perform. As usual, I can't take my eyes off her and the way she moves mesmerizes me. With each cut, my heart stops beating, and I pray that she makes it.

And she does. Because she's magnificent. My little ballerina soars through each test they put her through and goes to the very end with a handful of others. The temptation to let her know I'm thinking about her and with her during this stressful and difficult process makes me send a text: *Good luck. I'm pulling for you and wish you nothing but the best and for all your dreams to come true. You've got this, Sugar Plum.*

I know I shouldn't do it, but I really want her to know her success means the world to me. And, when she responds back with a fairy emoji, I burst out laughing.

In the interview portion, I lean forward, wishing I could hear her, but it's not like she's mic'd. The trio at the table seem interested in everything she says, ask questions and listen closely to her answers.

After a few final words, they dismiss her, and I sag back in my chair. The whole process is incredibly nerve-wracking, and I can't believe she's been through it several times. It's enough to age anyone ten years. Way worse than when I used to go through the audition process as an actor.

I'm so proud of her. Her grace and talent shine so brightly and ABC would be foolish to pass her up.

When I think the coast is clear, I get up, stretch and open the door. I spot Lizette talking to Taylor at the end of the hall and I duck back inside, waiting for them to finish. I don't want Taylor to see me. After they're done, I walk out and Lizette heads over.

"Thank you for inviting her to audition," I say. "And I appreciate you letting me watch."

"You're welcome. Thank you for referring her to us."

I smile, knowing Lizette is going to be coy and not reveal if they're going to accept her or not. "She's very talented. Am I right?"

"It takes more than talent to get into ABC," she says and my smile fades. "But, yes, you're right. I have a good feeling about her."

My smile returns and I nod. "Taylor Quinn is one in a million."

Lizette raises a brow. "So, why don't you tell her that, Chaz?" She gives me a wink, touches my arm as she passes by.

I ponder Lizette's question all the way home.

We had an amazing time together, but I practically forced her to sign that contract and be my fake girlfriend by offering her the one thing she wanted most-- a position in a prestigious ballet company.

What the hell is wrong with me? Am I that scared to have a real relationship? Did Sabrina mess me up that much or is some of this on me?

When my phone rings, I hit the button on my steering wheel to answer Cal's call. "Hi, Cal."

"Chaz, baby, I have got good news for you!"

"Oh?" I'm so wrapped up in thoughts of Taylor and how I screwed everything up that I haven't spent too much time thinking about movie roles.

"The studio wants to offer you the lead role!"

It's exactly what I want, but for some reason I really don't care anymore. "That's great," I say without a trace of enthusiasm in my voice.

"Chaz, did you hear me? We did it! They gave the Netflix kid the boot and you're going to play the lead like you wanted. Everything is peachy."

Peaches and cream. It's how Taylor smells and I think back to when I held her in my arms and breathed her sweet scent in deeply. *Fuck.* I've got it bad and I'm not sure what the hell to do about it.

"Chaz? Are you there?"

"I'm here."

I hear his annoyed sigh. "Okay, well, not exactly the reaction I expected, but take some time and let it sink in. Don't forget, you also have your first interview tonight. You have to be at the studio by 4pm for the 5pm taping."

"Shit." I completely forgot.

"You are on the way, right?"

"Uh, yeah. Headed over there right now." I check my rear-view mirror and switch lanes. Good thing I'm close and can get off the freeway and make it right in time.

"I sent you the list of questions they're going to ask so I hope you took a look."

"Sure did," I lie. I haven't checked my email in two days, but whatever. Interview questions are usually standard and avoid anything too personal. Luckily, I'm in a nice dress shirt and black pants already so I don't have to worry about a wardrobe change.

"Alright, well, call me afterward."

"Sure thing." I disconnect the call and realize how out of touch I've been with the rest of the world since Taylor stormed out. She's all I can think about, and I need to figure this out with her before I lose my damn mind.

Thirty minutes later, I'm in the green room and drinking a bottle of water, ready to go. They touch me up and put the mic in place. I should probably look over the questions for the interview, but I really don't have enough time. Nor do I care. If you've done one interview with a late-night talk show host, you've done 'em all.

A couple of minutes later, a production assistant appears to escort me to the stage. I wait at the edge, just out of sight, as the host does an intro. Then, the live audience bursts into applause and I walk out, forcing a smile and what I hope is a "I'm-so-happy-to-be-here look."

I wave to the crowd and shake hands with the host. "Great to see you, Chaz."

"Good to see you, Jimmy." I walk up a couple of steps and sit on the guest couch.

When the cheering and clapping dies down, Jimmy welcomes me to the show. "It's been a while since you've been here."

"I only come when you invite me, Jimmy," I say with a shrug and the audience chuckles.

"Oh, c'mon, you know you're always welcome. We missed you!"

Yeah, yeah. "Well, happy to be back."

"It appears you've been rather busy lately, though." He holds up a magazine and the image of me kissing Taylor in front of Cartier now fills every television screen across America. "Congratulations on your engagement."

The crowd claps and I feel like the rug just got yanked out from under me. When my heart starts beating again, I only smile. Words elude me right now and the charm I rely so heavily on in situations like this seems to have evaporated into thin air.

"Tell us a little about your mystery woman."

Oh, for fuck's sake. Why the hell didn't I look over the interview questions? Of course, there would be ones about Taylor. It shouldn't surprise me since I've been flaunting her all over from here to Europe. I clear my throat and look out. Past the cameras, past the audience. I picture Taylor-- her smooth, porcelain skin, bright blue eyes and flaming red hair. I think back over all of our kisses and conversations. Need and desire fill me as well as something else and it takes me a moment to recognize the foreign emotion that makes my chest tighten. Something that I only felt once before in my life, a very, very long time ago.

It's love.

I swallow hard. "Well, Jimmy, what can I say? She's perfect in every way and the moment I saw her, I fell hard and fast."

Aww's fill the air.

"Seems like it's been quite a whirlwind." He pulls out another magazine and shows more pictures of us in Paris. "This is a great shot outside here. Where are you?"

"The Palais Garnier. We saw the Paris Opera Ballet perform."

"Way to keep it classy, Chaz."

"Well, Taylor is a ballerina so getting to take her there was pretty amazing. Going there was like a dream for her and watching the way it made her light up was priceless. Something I'll never forget."

More aww's from the audience. *What did I say?*

"Well, you look so happy together and it's clear Chaz Stone has found love."

Warmth floods my face and, if I didn't know better, I must be blushing. I never blush.

"So, when's the wedding? I'm invited, right?"

The wedding? More like when will the news break that we're no longer together? The thought makes me sick. "I'll keep you posted," I say.

"Sounds good and I'm going to hold you to it."

Then, he moves on to another topic and I relax slightly. We talk for another ten minutes about movies and other inane things and then it's over. *Thank God,* I think, and sag in my chair when they cut to commercial. Jimmy thanks me for coming and I walk off the set.

On my way back home, I can't help but wonder if Taylor will see the interview when it airs later tonight. I have no idea what she will think. Hell, I don't even remember what I said. It's practically a blur.

I let myself in the front door and see Brand walk out of the kitchen. "Hey, bro," he says. "How'd the interview go?"

"Considering I completely forgot about it and then strolled in right on time, I'd say pretty damn good."

"What?"

I shake my head and feel so utterly lost. "Ever since our fight, I haven't been able to think about anything but Taylor." I run a hand through my hair and sigh.

"Call her."

"She won't talk to me, and I deserve it." I sit down on the couch, lean forward and drop my head in my hands. "I fucked up."

"Everybody fucks up at some point or another."

"It's more than that, though. I used her dream against her, to get my own way. What kind of person does that make me? I said Sabrina was a terrible person for cheating, but how am I any better?"

"You're nothing like Sabrina."

I take a deep breath. "I slept with her, Brand. When we were in Paris. I promised to keep it professional behind closed doors and the first thing I did was ply her with gifts and seduce her."

"I mean, I can't say I'm surprised. She's beautiful and there was obviously an attraction. But the thing I find odd is that you've never felt bad about seducing a woman before."

He's right. I've always embraced being single and somewhat of a playboy. So, what's so different with Taylor? "I think it's because she's so much younger and-" I abruptly stop talking. God, guilt is eating me up inside.

My brother waits for me to go on, but I can't even string the words together. I think the real issue here is I took her virginity when I had promised not to touch her in private. I feel like a liar and an asshole who tricked her and took advantage.

"I don't deserve her," I finally say.

Brand sits down next to me. "Bullshit. Maybe you didn't go about things in the most honorable or upfront way, but it's clear you care for her and that this is tearing you up inside."

"She was a virgin," I admit.

For a moment, he doesn't say anything. "Oh."

"Oh? That's all you got for me?"

"Well, assuming it was consensual-"

"Of course, it was," I snap.

"Then, I don't see a problem."

"I took advantage of her after promising not to and I feel like a piece of shit. She's way too good for me and sweet and innocent. And I hate myself for putting her through so much grief right before her audition."

"You went?"

I nod. "She didn't see me because I was in the private viewing room. But you should've seen her." I can't help the smile that lights me up from the inside then flows out. "She was magnificent. Made it all the way to the end." I'm bursting with pride and all I want to do is brag about how amazing she is and how proud I am. "Now they just have to make their decision."

"So do you."

"What do you mean?" I ask.

"C'mon, Chaz. I have never seen you so happy as you were with Taylor. It's pretty clear that you fell for her."

"I think I may have actually said that earlier during my interview with Jimmy."

Brand just shakes his head. "You have it bad, bro. Now you need to do something about it."

"Do what? She's done with me."

"Is she? Because I wouldn't be surprised if she's thinking about you, too."

"I saw her today and she was completely focused, definitely not crying over my dumb ass."

"Yeah, but that's over. Now, she's got time on her hands and I'm willing to bet my last dime that you're on her mind."

"I don't know."

"Fake or not, that relationship changed you for the better."

"If she is done, though…" My words trail off and my chest tightens. I can't even think about it. "It's almost better not knowing."

"Fuck, Chaz. When did you turn into such an angsty pile of mush? Go get your girl."

"I don't know if she ever really was my girl," I admit. I know Brand is right, though. I need to man-up and figure my shit out. "Guess there's only one way to find out."

"Damn," Brand says. "Remind me to never fall in love."

Yep. No more denying it. I love Taylor Quinn. Only problem is now I must beg her forgiveness and find the nerve to tell her.

And the worst thing is she may still want nothing to do with me after all is said and done.

Chapter Nineteen: Taylor

The moment I get home, I strip off my sweaty leotard, take a quick shower and just revel in the fact that I kicked ass today.

I get out, wrap myself up in a towel and realize when I go to look for something to where that I've finally done it. I've worn all of my clothes, and everything is officially dirty. *Hmm.* I scrounge through the mountain, lift a shirt and smell. *Nope, can't do it.* So, even though it's early, I put my boxers and t-shirt on that I normally wear to bed. Then, I pull my hair up in a damp, messy bun and grab my clothes basket.

Time to tackle my laundry.

Even though I'm dreading it, the good thing is that I have a couple hundred dollars' worth of quarters, thanks to Chaz. I try not to think too hard or too long about him as I fill the basket, grab detergent, a handful of change and head out to the laundry room.

But it's hard. *So damn hard.*

A man who I didn't even know two weeks ago has suddenly become my everything. How is that even possible? Especially for someone like me who is so focused on my dancing. I always said I didn't have time for a boyfriend, but Chaz proved me wrong. In more ways than one.

I walk into the laundry room and I'm so happy to see a few empty machines. The worst is when I finally decide to do laundry and so does everyone else in the complex. And Cody and Mason are the worst. They will start a load and not come back for ten hours. Sometimes, their stuff sits in the washing machine or dryer until the next day and even after we all complain, they just smile and apologize with a cute wink or quick hug.

Men, I think, and shake my head.

I separate my basket into two machines and hit start. Again, I wonder when I'm going to hear from ABC. The last two companies took weeks to respond and now I'm thinking that the longer you wait, the higher the probability the news will be bad. So, if I don't hear in the next day or two, I'll start panicking.

In the meantime, I'm going to stay positive and pray.

Back in my apartment, I get the next couple of loads ready then wander into the kitchen in search of food. I need to go to the grocery store. Like yesterday. That's another chore I tend to put off and now, as I look in my fridge, I wonder what to do for dinner.

Wait a second. I suddenly remember how much money I have in my bank account and decide to treat myself. I order a pizza and wish I had somebody to celebrate with. I text Jazz, but she responds back saying she's traveling and won't be back until the weekend. I'm sure Morgan is busy working like always, but I send her a text anyway. To my surprise, she says she's on her way over. I jump up and open the door as she walks up.

"Hey!"

"Hi, Tay," she says. "I'm so glad you invited me over for pizza because I just got home, I'm starving and have about two dollars in my bank account."

I give her a hug. "Well, I'm glad you could come over and celebrate. My ABC audition was today, and I have a really good feeling."

She gasps and claps. "I'm so happy for you."

"Even if I don't make it, I know that I did my absolute best."

"You'll make it."

"Lizette, the director, told me I knocked it out of the park."

We both squeal.

The pizza arrives fast. I hand Morgan a bottled water and we sit down at my little kitchen table and dig in. "You don't work tonight?" I ask.

She shakes her head. "Only one eight-hour shift today, thanks."

I notice the dark circles under her pretty blue eyes and nod. "You work too much."

"I don't have a choice," she says in a quiet voice.

"How's your mom doing?"

Morgan bites into the crust and suddenly stops chewing. A sheen of tears covers her eyes and I reach out a hand and squeeze her forearm. "Not good."

"I'm so sorry."

"The cancer has spread, and the bills are getting so high."

"Oh, Morgan," I say and get up to hug her. Morgan O'Connell is the sweetest person I know, and it hurts my heart that she's been going through so much lately. Suddenly, I remember the money Chaz put in my account. "I can give you some money. How much do you need?"

"That's sweet, Taylor, but we're talking about more money than either of us can afford. Like hundreds of thousands. But thank you." She swallows and takes another bite. "I don't want my problems to dampen the mood. We're celebrating for you so no more talking about me, okay?"

I nod. I hope things improve for her, but I have a feeling they're going to get worse before they get better.

After we eat, we go sit on the couch and I open a bottle of wine that I've been saving for a special occasion.

"Are you sure you want to waste it on me?" Morgan asks.

"Oh, stop! You're one of my best friends and I'm so glad you're here celebrating with me."

"You've worked your whole life for this moment and I'm so happy for you."

"Well, I haven't gotten the offer yet."

I finish pouring the wine and we lift our glasses. "To offers coming," Morgan says, and I clink my glass against hers.

"May they be very good ones," I add, and we each take a sip.

"So, what's going on with Chaz?" she asks. "Last I heard, you were raving about Paris, falling in love and had a rock the size of Mt. Everest on your finger."

I look down at my bare finger and tell myself not to cry. "We broke things off."

"What? Why?"

"It was all fake and I found out the real reason why he came up to me. He didn't like me, Morgan. His friend bet him that he couldn't sleep with me. That's how it all started and then it led to that stupid contract."

"I'm so sorry."

"Yeah, me, too." I swirl the wine around in my glass. "I really thought things were becoming...I don't know...real. But I was wrong. I had my Cinderella moment and then the clock struck midnight."

My phone rings and I glance down. "It's Jazz."

"Put her on speaker."

"Hey, Jazz," we both say at once and laugh.

"Heyyy! Who's there?"

"It's Morgan. We're celebrating with pizza and wine because our girl here just kicked some butt earlier at her audition for ABC."

A loud whoop comes over the line. "Congrats, Tay. I'm so happy for you."

"Thanks. Hopefully, I hear something good tomorrow or the next day."

"Well, you may hear something good in a few hours."

Morgan and I exchange a look. "What do you mean?" I ask.

"I'm in New York and just happened to turn on the Late Show and guess who's on?"

My stomach drops. "Who?"

"Chaz Stone and let's just say he talks about you."

"*What?*" Is she kidding? What in the world would he say about me?

"Yep. I can't believe you're three hours behind. You're not going to believe what he says. I want you to see it right now!"

"She can," Morgan says.

"How?" I ask.

"Jazz, do you have a rewind button on your remote?"

"Oh, shit, Morgan you're a freaking genius."

Suddenly, I'm so nervous that a tremble runs through my body.

"Okay, I'm going to call you right back on video chat."

We hang up and all the coolness I've been able to maintain vanishes. "Oh, my God, Morgan. I don't know if I can watch this."

"You're watching," she says, and my phone starts ringing again with Jasmine's face on the screen.

I slide the bar over and I'm nervous. Like really freaking nervous. I have no idea what to expect and my heart is about to fall out of my ass.

"Okay," Jazz says. "I've got it right when he comes out. Are you ready?"

I nod and she hits play and focuses her camera on the large screen television in her hotel room. After a quick introduction, Chaz strolls into view looking happy and laidback. He waves to the crowd, and they cheer. He shakes hands with the host and sits on the couch.

God, he looks so handsome.

When the applause finally stops, Jimmy says, "It's been a while since you've been here."

"I only come when you invite me, Jimmy."

"Oh, c'mon, you know you're always welcome. We missed you!"

"Well, happy to be back."

He's so charming. Always with the right answers, the right look, the right body language. He exudes confidence, yet not arrogance. That's something I always liked about him.

"Okay, here it comes," Jasmine says.

"It appears you've been rather busy lately, though," Jimmy comments and then lifts a magazine with the image of Chaz kissing me in front of the Cartier store. "Congratulations on your engagement."

"Oh, my God," I whisper, unable to look away.

The crowd claps and it seems like the comment takes him by surprise because for a moment, he doesn't say anything. But I see the emotions flash across his face.

"Tell us a little about your mystery woman."

Chaz clears his throat and I lean forward, wondering what in the world he's going to say. He gazes past the camera; the audience and it feels like he's looking right at me. Talking directly to me. He takes a moment and then a small smile curves the edge of his mouth. "Well, Jimmy, what can I say? She's perfect in every way and the moment I saw her, I fell hard and fast."

Aww's fill the air in the studio audience, and I cover my mouth with a hand. Does he mean it or is he just playing a role still? Pretending for the sake of the audience and viewers?

"Seems like it's been a whirlwind." Jimmy pulls out another magazine and shows more pictures of us in Paris. "This is a great shot outside here. Where are you?"

The Palais Garnier.

"The Palais Garnier. We saw the Paris Opera Ballet perform."

"Way to keep it classy, Chaz."

"Well, Taylor is a ballerina so getting to take her there was pretty amazing. Going there was like a dream for her and watching the way it made her light up was priceless. Something I'll never forget."

More aww's from the audience.

"Well, you look so happy together and it's clear Chaz Stone has found love."

It's a little hard to tell, but I swear he blushes.

"So, when's the wedding? I'm invited, right?"

I suck in a breath. *The wedding?*

"I'll keep you posted," Chaz says.

"Sounds good and I'm going to hold you to it."

Jasmine hits pause and I feel Morgan looking at me. "I don't know what to say," I murmur.

"I think your man misses you," Jasmine says.

"Does he, though?" I ask. "He said all this on television, but not to me. He's an actor and he put on a show. It's what he does."

"When's the last time you talked to him?" Morgan asks.

"Technically, I haven't spoken to him since our fight. I've ignored all of his texts and calls until today. He sent me a text right before my interview."

"What did it say?" Jasmine asks.

"Good luck."

"Just good luck? Tell me exactly what it said."

I don't even have to pull up my texts because his words burned themselves into my heart. "He wrote: *Good luck. I'm pulling for you and wish you nothing but the best and for all your dreams to come true. You've got this, Sugar Plum.*"

"Oh, my God!" Jasmine cries.

"That was so sweet. He totally misses you!" Morgan exclaims.

"You think?" I am so confused and don't know what to think.

"Taylor Quinn, you need to return his damn phone calls or y'all aren't ever gonna be able to get your shit together!"

I give a half-laugh, half-sob because these girls are giving me hope. Suddenly, tears are streaming down my face, and I ask Jazz if she will rewind the interview so I can watch it again. The moment it ends, a text from Chaz pops up on my phone.

Chapter Twenty: Chaz

After talking to Brand, I decide to end this once and for all. With a deep breath, I sit down and pull up my texts to Taylor. Her little fairy emoji makes me smile and I begin to tap out a message: *I hope your audition went well and I'd love to hear about it. Are you busy right now? I just sent a car to pick you up and if you will give me a chance, I'd like to explain some things. If you don't come over, I won't bother you again.*

With my heart in my throat, I hit send.

This is it; I think. Shit, I've never been so nervous in my life. Will she come over? What if she doesn't? How the hell am I going to survive without Taylor in my life? A million thoughts fly through my head, and I look down at my phone and wait. The minutes drag by and after ten minutes, there's still no response.

She's not coming.

The thought is like a punch to the gut. I let out a breath and rub my fists against my eyes. They feel tired and gritty. I've never been good at waiting for anything, and patience is a virtue that I possess little of, so this kills me. My knee bounces, my nerves feel taut, and I realize I'm sweating.

Great, I think, and head down to my room to change. If she comes, God willing, I don't want to greet her with pit stains and smelling like I just worked out. I change into something more casual and sit down on the edge of my bed. I'm clutching my phone like a lifeline and open my text to Taylor again. No response.

Fucking fuck.

What does that mean? Did she see it and think screw you? Is she busy and hasn't seen it yet? Is she sitting there, debating whether to get in the car?

I don't know what to think and I am wound so tight right now. Like a rubber band stretched to its limit, ready to snap. I glance at my watch and realize 25 minutes have passed. The little bit of hope I had begun to crumble.

Maybe she just saw the text. Maybe she's in the car, on her way over. I figure it should take her around a half an hour to get here from her place. If she left right away, she'll be here in five minutes. I pop up and head into the bathroom to brush my teeth and splash some water on my face.

She must come. Taylor wouldn't just ignore me. *Would she?*

Well, she's been doing a pretty good job of ignoring me since our fight. Hell, I know I deserve it, but it hurts. Wanting Taylor and not having her hurts more than anything ever has before. More than when Sabrina cheated on me, more than my divorce, more than being looked over for the lead and being offered the grandpa role instead.

I walk out to the living room and begin to pace back and forth. It's been almost 40 minutes. Just as I'm about to drop down on the couch and feel sorry for myself, there's a knock at the door and my heart slams against my chest.

Thank God, I think, and rush over. I throw the door open, ready to fall at her feet and beg her forgiveness, but it isn't Taylor. It's John.

"Hey, Chaz."

It's like a giant boot just crushed my last bit of hope and I motion for him to come inside.

"Don't look so happy to see me."

"Sorry, I just thought you were someone else."

"I wanted to apologize for the other night. Brand told me what happened. I shouldn't have said anything about the bet in front of her."

I sigh. "It doesn't matter. It's over."

"Are you okay with that?"

"No, but what am I supposed to do?"

"Fight for her."

"I sent a car to pick her up 45 minutes ago. Even with traffic…" my voice trails off. "If she wanted to see me and work things out, she'd be here."

"So, she could be on her way over here right now?"

"Yeah. I mean, maybe."

"Dude." John slaps my shoulder. "She'll come."

I just shake my head. "It's not looking that way."

"Look, I didn't realize how much you liked this girl. To be honest, I thought the whole thing was a joke until I saw her here. The way you decorated that whole room and took her to Paris. You've never done anything like that. And I saw the way you looked at her. I should've known."

"It was never a joke. The moment I laid eyes on her, before the bet, I was interested."

"I heard about your interview earlier today."

"Fuck. I can't believe I said all that on national TV. I must be crazy."

"Yeah, crazy in love."

"This is humiliating."

"I guess the good news is half the country already saw it and it's over."

"That's the good news?"

When there's a knock on the door, we both look. "Actually," John says. "I think that might be the good news."

My heart kicks up and we walk over to the door. I see a flash of red hair through beveled glass, and I nearly stop breathing.

"Good luck," John says. He opens the door, sees Taylor and leans closer to murmur, "Be gentle with him." Then, he heads down the drive to his car.

Taylor looks back over at me and I am so happy to see her. But I'm wary. The look on her face is hard to read. "Hi," I say.

"Hi."

"C'mon, in." She walks inside and I force myself to hold back and not reach out for her when all I want to do is drag her into my arms and ask her to forgive me for being so stupid. "Thanks for coming over."

She nods and I motion for her to sit down on the couch.

"I wanted to start by saying I'm sorry."

"Chaz-"

"No, please, hear me out. I was an idiot, a complete jerk to take such a stupid bet. I felt like I had something to prove, though, and I shouldn't have let it get under my skin. Not my friends, not the studio, not the media. I fucked up. I know that now and, to top it all off, I took advantage of the situation and had Lang make that stupid contract."

Taylor doesn't say a word, just listens.

"I thought that by having you on my arm, people would see me as relevant again and look at me how they used to when I was young and on top. But it became so much more than that, Taylor. You're young and vibrant and that's what initially drew me to you, but then I got to know you." I pause, trying to read her reaction.

"Go on," she says.

She's listening so I take that as a good sign and continue. "Even though I planned for Paris to only be a publicity blitz, it turned into so much more. You need to know that everything that happened there was real. All of our time together, everything I said and did…they weren't lies, and it wasn't a show."

I can see the emotion flicker through her blue eyes, and I take a chance and reach for her hand. "I fell in love with you there, Taylor."

When she squeezes my hand, it gives me hope. "I fell in love with you, too," she says in a soft voice.

"And now?"

"And now, I'm hopelessly, head over heels for you."

Relief pours through me. "Do you know how much I've missed you?"

"A lot?"

"More than that."

"Enough to go on TV and tell the whole world that you fell hard and fast for little 'ol me?" she teases.

"How did you know that? The show doesn't air for another couple of hours."

"Oh, I have my ways." I raise a brow. "And that includes a friend on the East coast right now."

"Minx," I say. My gaze drops to her mouth, and I realize just how much I've missed kissing her. "Your audition went well."

"Is that a question or a statement?"

I take a deep breath and hope she doesn't get pissed all over again. "I was there in the viewing room. I didn't want you to see me or get upset or lose focus. But I had to be there for you, Taylor."

She looks surprised at first, but then her expression softens, and she smiles. "It's funny because it's like I felt your presence."

"You did?"

She nods. "Yeah. It helped me focus and do my best."

"You kicked ass is what you did."

She gives a little laugh. "How long were you cooped up in that little room?"

"All day."

"You stayed the whole time?" she asks in disbelief.

"Of course."

For a moment, she's speechless. "No one's ever believed in me like you, Chaz."

"I'll always believe in you, Sugar Plum."

When her eyes tear up, I brush a thumb over her cheek. "Don't cry."

"But they're happy tears."

"C'mere," I say and pull her into my arms. I press a kiss to her forehead, drop one at the corner of her eye and taste a tear as it rolls down her cheek. Then, I drop my mouth to her sweet lips. Kissing Taylor is like coming home. She's my person, the one who makes me want to be a better man. No one has ever made me feel that before.

It's been too long and the heat between us builds fast. Our tongues tangle in a desperate dance and I hold her face in my hands, deepening the kiss. When we finally pull apart, chests heaving, there's nothing I want more than Taylor in my bed. And I'm going to spend all night showing her how happy I am to have her there.

I scoop her up off the couch and head back to my bedroom. I really hope that Brand and the entourage stay away tonight because I am going to be occupied until the sun comes up. And I really don't want them hearing my little ballerina's screaming orgasms because I plan to give her plenty. I kick the door shut and stand her on the bed in front of me.

"Are you in your pajamas?" I ask, looking at her t-shirt and boxers.

She nods. "I was in the middle of doing laundry and ran out of clean clothes."

"Did you use my quarters?" I ask, nuzzling her neck.

"Mm-hmm. I always wait until the last minute and never have any."

"Stay with me and I'll make sure you always have quarters, Sugar Plum."

"Oh, really?"

"Among other things."

She leans her head to the side, giving me better access and I suck on the sensitive skin there. "Like what?" she murmurs.

"Anything and everything your heart desires." I feel her smile and make quick work of removing her boxers and t-shirt. "Oh, and plenty of orgasms."

She chuckles and we pull my clothes off and then I stretch her out beneath me. Skin to skin, I relish the feel of her curves and begin to explore every last one with my lips, tongue and hands. Taylor moans, arching beneath me, as I draw a rosy-tipped nipple into my mouth. I plan on worshipping her all night, so I hope she's ready.

"You're not going to get any sleep tonight," I warn her and move to her other breast.

Her fingers rake through my hair. "I'm not tired."

"Good because we have some lost time to make up."

I lick my way down to her stomach and swirl my tongue around her navel. Then, I spread her thighs and sink my face into her hot, wet centre. My fiery redhead bucks her hips and cries out as I work her up into a frenzy.

"Chaz…" she says, voice harsh with need. She's writhing and twisting the sheets up in her fist.

I pull her throbbing nub into my mouth and suck hard enough to make her splinter. Taylor cries out, the powerful release making her entire body spasm. I kiss my way back up her body and our gaze's lock.

She lets out a shaky sigh and my mouth edges up. "You're really too good at that," she says in a husky voice.

"I'm good at a lot of stuff and I'm going to show you all of my best moves."

"Promise?" she asks and drops a hand between our bodies, wrapping her slender fingers around my cock.

"Jesus," I hiss as her hand begins to stroke me. I'm hard as steel and aching to be inside her, but I hold off for as long as I can. But Taylor is in more of a hurry and when she starts to slide down my body, I pull her back up. "When I come, it's going to be deep inside you."

I reach over and grab a condom from the nightstand drawer.

"Can I?" Taylor asks. When she holds a hand out, I hand her the foil packet. "I've never done this before."

My eyes slide shut, and I want to groan. God, her innocence turns me on and I help her roll the protection on and then move between her legs, spreading them further apart, giving myself better access to that sweet, dripping centre.

As I slide inside, stretching her tight, wet body, she starts making those sexy sounds at the back of her throat and I'm done. I thrust deep and she cries out, lifting her hips, and I guide her body, moving it with mine. Faster and harder, until we're both soaring with pleasure.

Our gazes connect and we both shatter in a mind-blowing climax at the same time and cry out each other's name. A powerful shudder ripples through our locked bodies and the explosion leaves us both panting hard. I roll over and drop my head down on the pillow beside her and all we can do is stare at each other, waiting for our hearts to slow down, trying to make sense of this deep connection we have.

"Are you okay?" I ask and tuck a fiery strand of hair behind her ear.

She nods. "Is it always this intense?"

"Only with you."

She smiles and lays a dainty hand over my thundering heart. "Good." Then, her blue eyes cloud over a bit. "What about your ex-wife?"

"Sabrina? What about her?"

"Why did you get divorced?"

"Because I found her in our bed with another man."

"I can't imagine how much that must've hurt," she says.

I cover her hand with mine. "I knew our marriage was falling apart, but I still felt betrayed. And ever since I avoided anything serious with a woman. It just wasn't worth the risk." I meet her gaze. "Until you." I lace my fingers through hers. "You're the best thing that ever happened to me and I love you, Taylor," I whisper. "So very much."

"I love you, too," she says and leans over to meet my lips in a slow, searing kiss.

And, then we spend the rest of the night showing each other just how much.

Epilogue: Taylor

Waking up in Chaz's strong, warm arms is the greatest feeling in the world. I snuggle up against his chest and sigh. Nothing has ever felt so right.

"Morning," he says, voice rough with sleep.

"Good morning," I say.

The bright sun shines in the window and I'm guessing it must be around 11am. I'm not sure we got more than a few hours of sleep, but I am not complaining. In fact, I have never been happier. I sit up, pulling the sheet with me, and tuck it beneath my arms. "You weren't joking when you said you were going to show me all of your best moves. And, you've got quite a lot of them, sir."

"And they're all reserved for you, mademoiselle. But don't sell yourself short."

I raise a brow.

"I knew you were flexible," he says, "but, Christ Almighty, you're like a damn contortionist." He lays on his back and watches me like a big, lazy cat. Then, he trails a finger down my arm, and I get goosebumps. "I may not ever let you out of my bed."

"I will need to eat at some point," I say. As if on cue, my stomach growls.

Chaz sits up. "I guess I can let you out long enough to have some breakfast," he teases. "We need to keep your strength up. So, you can show me some more of that bendy thing you do."

"You're insatiable," I say and swat at his arm.

He growls and then slaps a hand over my rear. "C'mon. Let's see what we can find in the kitchen."

Chaz slides on a pair of loose-fitting pajama bottoms and I pull my t-shirt and boxers on and, before long, we find ourselves in his big kitchen, sitting at the island on stools. A veritable feast is spread out before us from fresh fruit to cereal to bacon, sausage and pancakes dripping in syrup.

I take a sip of orange juice. "I think this is more than enough to recharge me."

"I hope so because I have plans for you later."

I study him over the rim of my glass-- from the top of his burnished gold head down to his very blue eyes to the whiskers covering his lower face. His tan, bare chest makes my stomach do crazy somersaults and those bottoms he's wearing are indecently low, bringing color to my cheeks as I recall all the naughty, delightfully sublime things we did to each other last night.

One thing is clear: I don't ever want to be without this man again.

"What are you thinking?" he asks and pops a strawberry in his mouth.

"I guess I'm just thinking over this crazy journey we've had. That even though everything started as a farce, somewhere along the way it became real. And, here I am, on the verge of my happily ever after."

"On the verge?"

"I really want to believe it'll happen and you're the only person I'd want as my forever."

A funny look comes over his face. "I might've been married before, but I've never been anyone's forever. No one's stuck around long enough."

"I'll stick around. If you want me to."

Chaz turns to face me and pulls my stool closer, so I'm trapped between his long legs. "I'd like that." He runs a finger down my nose and gives me that megawatt, devastating smile that I've missed so much. "I'll even do your laundry, Sugar Plum."

I laugh. "I'm going to hold you to that."

"On one condition," he says. He reaches into a pocket in his pajama bottoms and pulls out the Cartier engagement ring we chose in Paris. "We do this right."

My mouth drops when Chaz pulls me off the stool and then goes down on one knee.

"Taylor Quinn, my feisty little ballerina, I know our journey together wasn't always what it seemed, but, to me, it was always real. I knew from the moment I saw you-- saw that spark, energy and determination. You have so much heart and give everything you do 110 percent. I love your passion and the way you pursue your dream. You made me believe in love again and that's something I never thought could happen. So, thank you. I hope you know I'm never letting you go so you can say yes right now and make this easy or-"

"Yes."

"You'll marry me?"

"Yes, yes, yes, yes, yes!" I cry.

We both laugh and he slips the ring on my finger. It feels right and so good to have it back where it belongs. I pull Chaz up and lean into him, and his mouth captures mine in a kiss that promises so many wonderful things to come.

Later that afternoon, Chaz and I sit on the couch and talk about the future. He wants me to move in right away and it's such a big step, but I think I'm ready. Because, honestly, there's nowhere on Earth that I'd rather be than here with him. And the idea of waking up every morning in his arms seals the deal.

"I'll hire the movers," he says, lifts my hand up to his mouth and drags his lips from one knuckle to the next. "Get you settled in here by next weekend." His tongue glides between my fingers, bright blue eyes never leaving mine.

Oh, my man is steamy, I think, as a shot of desire hits me. It doesn't take much and before I know it, our clothes are gone and I'm in his arms. After a vigorous romp, I fall back against his hard chest and pull his hands up under my chin. The rest of the day is spent much the same way and we christen every room in every way possible and take a break every now and then to eat and regain some energy.

After having some fun on his desk later that evening, my gaze lands on the contract which sits on the corner. When he notices me looking at it, he grabs it. Then, he walks over to the fireplace, tosses it on the grate and lights a match. I walk over and wrap my arms around his waist and together we watch it burn.

"I remember when I asked for clarification, and you told me to think of you more like a Daddy figure. Someone who would take care of me and make sure I have everything I need." He waits for me to continue. "That part was okay," I admit in a low voice.

"You like that? Being taken care of?" His arms tighten around me.

I nod and tilt my head back so I can look up into his eyes. "I know the contract is gone, but can we maybe add a little something to that part?"

He arches a brow. "And, what's that?"

"That you take care of my laundry, too?"

The look on his face is priceless and I burst out laughing and wriggle away from him. I squeal as he chases me across the room then catches me and sweeps me up into his arms. "What is your deal with doing laundry?" he asks and nips my chin.

"I hate it. With a passion."

"Hmm," he murmurs and captures my mouth in a slow, deep kiss. "You just gave me an idea."

"What?" I ask in a breathless voice.

"You haven't seen my laundry room yet. Maybe you won't be so averse to it if I show you how much fun we can have when it hits the spin cycle."

I never thought about it that way before.

"Baby, I'm going to have you wanting to do laundry every day," he murmurs and then carries me down to his washing machine.

He's right, too. I don't mind doing laundry anymore. In fact, as long as Chaz is there to help me, I kind of enjoy it. Thoroughly.

The call from the American Ballet Company comes the next day, two days after my audition. I'm so nervous when I answer, and Chaz takes my hand in his and squeezes. His support means the world to me and no matter what happens, I know I'm going to be okay.

When they invite me to be a part of the company, I am speechless at first. Then, I thank Lizette profusely and tell her how honored and excited I am. Of course, I will start at the bottom as part of the corps and then work my way up by proving I have what it takes to be a soloist and eventually a principal. *A Prima Ballerina.*

But I've got my foot in the door and I am now going to dance for one of the most prestigious ballet companies in the country. It's beyond anything I could've hoped for, and I can't stop smiling. Lizette and I talk for a few minutes and she fill me in on things I need to know regarding practice, class and rehearsals.

Then, she slyly asks me how Chaz is doing.

"He's great," I say and squeeze his hand. "And, right here, looking at me like he's about to burst with pride."

Lizette chuckles and invites us to have dinner with her next week. After I hang up, Chaz sweeps me up and spins me around in a circle. "Do you know how damn proud I am of you?" He sets me down. "I have a little something for you."

"For me?"

He nods. "A surprise. Hang on."

Then, with a mysterious smile, he disappears down the hall. I have no idea what he could possibly have for me and there's nothing I need except him. I sit down on the couch and wait. He's back in under a minute and carries a box wrapped up with a big pink bow. He hands it to me with that trademark, killer smile of his. "Congratulations, Taylor."

Very carefully, I pull off the bow and unwrap the paper to reveal a shoebox. But not just any shoebox. *A Chanel shoebox.* My eyes go wide, and I look over at him. "What is this?"

"Just a little something I had specially made for my little ballerina."

Heart in my throat, I lift the lid, fold back the classic double-C tissue paper back and gasp. "Oh, Chaz," I exclaim and lift a pair of gorgeous baby-pink Chanel pointe shoes. The small signature C's are sewn onto the side and the elegant emblem is dotted through the pink satin ribbons. "These are beautiful."

"You like them?"

"I love them!"

"Try them on," he says and takes the box off my lap, tossing it aside.

I slip the beautiful, handmade ballet shoes on, tie the fancy ribbons around my ankles and stand up to model them. I go up on my right toes, lift my left leg back and extend my body in a graceful arabesque. The shoes aren't broken in and feel untried, but it doesn't matter. If I'm going to actually dance in them, I'll have to put them through the wringer and do some damage to make them mold to my feet and be comfortable.

And, I don't have the heart to tell Chaz that a lot of times hammers and files are used in the process.

But, in the meantime, I do a little pirouette and then take a bow.

As I look at Chaz watching me, I realize that I have never been happier in my life. "It's kind of strange when a dream finally comes true," I say and look down at the diamond ring that sparkles on my finger. "And I feel like I've had two happen-- I am in the corps de ballet at ABC and I am engaged to the most amazing man in the world."

Chaz gets up and walks over to me. His hands slide over my hips, and he pulls me close. "You're my dream come true, Sugar Plum," he says. Then, he leans down and kisses me. And, as I melt against him, I know that our future together is going to be very sweet indeed.

Printed in Great Britain
by Amazon